BRA[illegible]ACK

Joe wandered back onstage and found Frank and Callie. "Hi," he called as he approached them.

Suddenly they heard someone shouting from the other end of the stage. Joe turned to see Buddy Death pointing at him.

"Hey, punk!" Buddy yelled as he marched over to Joe. "What're you doing on my stage? I want you out of here, or there's going to be trouble!" He pushed Joe in the chest.

"Take it easy, man," Frank said. "What's the matter with you?"

"I want both of you out of here!" Buddy shouted. Snarling with rage, he reached for a nearby pile of scrap lumber and grabbed a two-by-four. Brandishing it like a baseball bat, he advanced on the Hardys.

"Watch out, Joe!" Callie screamed. "He's going to kill you!"

Books in THE HARDY BOYS CASEFILES™ Series

#1 DEAD ON TARGET
#2 EVIL, INC.
#3 CULT OF CRIME
#4 THE LAZARUS PLOT
#5 EDGE OF DESTRUCTION
#6 THE CROWNING TERROR
#7 DEATHGAME
#8 SEE NO EVIL
#9 THE GENIUS THIEVES
#10 HOSTAGES OF HATE
#11 BROTHER AGAINST BROTHER
#12 PERFECT GETAWAY
#13 THE BORGIA DAGGER
#14 TOO MANY TRAITORS
#15 BLOOD RELATIONS
#16 LINE OF FIRE
#17 THE NUMBER FILE
#18 A KILLING IN THE MARKET
#19 NIGHTMARE IN ANGEL CITY
#20 WITNESS TO MURDER
#21 STREET SPIES
#22 DOUBLE EXPOSURE
#23 DISASTER FOR HIRE
#24 SCENE OF THE CRIME
#25 THE BORDERLINE CASE
#26 TROUBLE IN THE PIPELINE
#27 NOWHERE TO RUN
#28 COUNTDOWN TO TERROR
#29 THICK AS THIEVES
#30 THE DEADLIEST DARE
#31 WITHOUT A TRACE
#32 BLOOD MONEY
#33 COLLISION COURSE
#34 FINAL CUT
#35 THE DEAD SEASON
#36 RUNNING ON EMPTY
#37 DANGER ZONE
#38 DIPLOMATIC DECEIT
#39 FLESH AND BLOOD
#40 FRIGHT WAVE
#41 HIGHWAY ROBBERY
#42 THE LAST LAUGH
#43 STRATEGIC MOVES
#44 CASTLE FEAR
#45 IN SELF-DEFENSE
#46 FOUL PLAY
#47 FLIGHT INTO DANGER
#48 ROCK 'N' REVENGE

Available from ARCHWAY Paperbacks

ROCK 'N' REVENGE

FRANKLIN W. DIXON

AN ARCHWAY PAPERBACK
Published by POCKET BOOKS
New York London Toronto Sydney Tokyo Singapore

This book is a work of fiction. Names, characters, places and incidents are either the product of the author's imagination or are used fictitiously. Any resemblance to actual events or locales or persons, living or dead, is entirely coincidental.

AN ARCHWAY PAPERBACK *Original*

An Archway Paperback published by
POCKET BOOKS, a division of Simon & Schuster
1230 Avenue of the Americas, New York, NY 10020

Produced by Mega-Books of New York, Inc.

ISBN: 0-671-70045-6

First Archway Paperback printing February 1991

10 9 8 7 6 5 4 3 2 1

Cover art by Brian Kotzky

Printed in the U.S.A.

IL 7+

ROCK 'N' REVENGE

Chapter 1

"CANCELED? WHAT DO YOU MEAN, the ski trip's been canceled?" Joe Hardy shouted into the receiver.

He listened for a few moments and then slammed down the phone. "Rats!" Joe's blue eyes flashed angrily.

"What's the matter, Joe?" asked his older brother, Frank.

Joe glanced over at Frank, who was filling a camera bag at the far end of the kitchen. Frank had a long telephoto lens in one hand and the camera body in the other.

Frank Hardy's dark, lean form contrasted with Joe's muscular body and blond hair. The two brothers' personalities were as different as their looks. Frank was the calm, logical brother, while Joe often acted impulsively. Yet it was these very differences that made the pair such a successful team of detectives.

"That was Mr. Abrams, the ski club advisor," Joe said, disappointed. "He says the spring break ski trip's been canceled."

"What happened?"

"A warm front melted all the powder off the slopes, and no one's making snow because it's too warm."

"Why not come to the sports arena with Callie and me, then, and watch them set up for the Buddy Death concert?"

"Buddy Death?" Joe said scornfully. "He stinks!"

Frank shrugged and picked up the camera bag. "Suit yourself. I'm going to pick up Callie and head over there now."

Frank walked toward the back door, whistling slightly off-key. Joe watched him go, still sulking. Spring break was his last chance that year to ski at Snow Valley. He'd been looking forward to tackling Suicide Slide one more time that season.

The kitchen door slammed, snapping Joe out of his reverie. "Hey, Frank! Wait up!" he called.

"The place seems kind of empty with Mom and Aunt Gertrude away," he admitted, joining his brother in their black customized van.

"Even Buddy Death has to be more fun than hanging around the kitchen by myself."

Frank grinned as he started the van's engine and pulled out of the driveway. He was glad to see Joe acting like himself again. "Yeah. Who knows when Dad'll be back from San Francisco."

Joe sighed and nodded. Fenton Hardy was a well-known private detective whose work often took him away from Bayport.

After a short drive they pulled up at the house of Frank's steady girlfriend, Callie Shaw. Frank tapped the horn twice, and the front door quickly opened. Callie waved and ran out to the van, her pretty face glowing with excitement.

"Hi, Joe!" Callie said. "I wasn't expecting to see you today."

"My plans got canceled. Guess it's your lucky day," Joe kidded.

"It sure is!" Callie said. "Doing this piece on Buddy Death is my big chance with the Bayport *Times*. If I do a good job, the features editor promised me regular work, which shouldn't be a problem with Frank Hardy, ace photographer, at my side."

Frank laughed and threw the van into gear. "What kind of background stuff did you dig up on Buddy Death?" he asked as he stepped on the accelerator.

"Not much. He hasn't been on the heavy

metal scene that long, and, of course, this is his first national tour."

"I don't get what all the fuss is about," Joe said. "You know heavy metal's my music, but I think Buddy stinks."

"Buddy's last LP shot up to number one and never came down. He's got an enormous following," said Frank. "I'm not really into heavy metal, but he's okay."

The van topped the next hill, and the oval-shaped Bayport Sports Arena, its white dome gleaming, seemed to fill the horizon.

As they pulled into the parking lot Joe noticed several helicopters circling overhead. On their sides were the emblems of three major TV networks. "What are they looking at?" Joe asked.

"That," said Callie. She pointed at the main entrance to the arena. It was jam-packed with teenagers in ripped-up clothes, heavy make-up, and brightly colored hair. They milled about excitedly, chanting Buddy's name. One fan was playing Buddy's music on a gigantic boom box while others danced in frantic circles to the wild, angry beat.

"The concert's not for two days, and they're already camped out," said Frank. "I told you, Joe. Buddy has the Midas touch."

After parking the van, the trio checked in with arena security and were allowed into one of the four wide, high-ceilinged access tunnels that led directly onto the huge floor of the arena.

"Wow. This *is* major," Joe said as they cleared the tunnel. A huge stage had already been partly erected across the north end of the space. A crew of roadies was speedily assembling a network of steel crossbeams and pillars to support the apron of the stage, which extended in a half circle into the audience.

"Look up there," said Frank.

Joe raised his eyes and spotted members of the lighting crew moving along narrow catwalks that stretched across the center of the enormous dome and ran along the edges.

"What are those towers for?" Callie pointed to the tall steel structures on either side of the stage. "They look like giant Tinkertoys."

"They support the speakers," Joe told her. "For a concert this size they'll need enough speakers to knock down the back wall." Joe watched the crew, impressed by the way each person moved thirty feet above the ground, supported only by a small harness.

"The tour must cost a fortune," said Callie.

"You kids don't know the half of it." Joe turned to see a short, bald, middle-aged man in gray slacks, a yellow- and red-striped sweater, and dark sunglasses lounging beside a pile of equipment.

He walked over to Callie and the Hardys.

"You kids got a pass? This shindig's not open to the public."

"I'm Callie Shaw from the Bayport *Times*," Callie said.

"Oh. That's different. I'm Syd Schacht. I'm the promoter of this tour." He gave Callie a toothy smile and shook her hand. "Who're your friends?"

"I'm Frank Hardy, Mr. Schacht. I'm Callie's photographer."

"And I'm Joe Hardy. I'm just along for the ride. I hope that's okay."

"Sure!" Schacht replied. "Just stay out of everyone's way." Then he frowned and muttered to himself, "Hardy, Hardy—why does that name sound familiar?"

"Maybe you've heard of their dad," said Callie. "Fenton Hardy, the detective?"

"Oh, yeah!" Schacht grinned from behind the sunglasses. "He did an investigation for a friend of mine a few years ago. Saved him a pile of money. Well, it's good to know we've got friends in high places." He laughed loudly and slapped Frank on the back.

"Frank and Joe are detectives, too," Callie said. Schacht just nodded.

"Is Buddy around yet?" Callie asked.

Schacht pointed to a shiny black motor home parked near access tunnel C at the opposite end of the arena. Joe was surprised to see a motor home inside the dome, but he realized that the access tunnel they had come through had ceilings high enough to accommodate even big equipment trucks.

"He's in there with his manager, Bobby Mellor," said Schacht. "Poor guy spent all morning doing interviews, and he's feeling out of it. Maybe you should talk to the rest of the band first. Come on, I'll introduce you."

Frank and Callie followed Schacht toward the stage. "I'll catch you later, Frank," Joe said. "I want to check out this operation."

"Keep your head up, kid," said Schacht. "There's a lot of steel flying through the air today."

Joe waved in acknowledgment and turned toward one of the sound towers, where a team of twenty roadies was passing six-foot lengths of steel pipe upward in a human chain. Joe was intrigued by the way the roadies assembled each level of the tower from the corners, bolting the diagonal supports to the corner posts.

After a few minutes Joe wandered over to look at Buddy Death's black motor home. Stylized white skulls with the initials BDB on the forehead—the logo for the Buddy Death Band—were painted on both sides of the motor home. Another one decorated the hood.

Suddenly Joe grew aware of the sound of someone singing and playing an acoustic guitar. It was a beautiful sound—high and clear.

Nothing like the sound of Buddy Death's band members.

Curious, Joe followed the sound through access tunnel C to a side door and peeked outside. He spotted the singer immediately.

She was a tall, slender girl with auburn hair that fell in waves past her shoulders. She was dressed in a white cotton blouse and a colorful peasant skirt even though it was still wintry. She was so intent on her playing that she didn't notice Joe approach.

"Hi," he said, flashing her a friendly grin as she noticed him and stopped singing. "Don't stop on my account. You play beautifully."

The auburn-haired girl blushed and lowered her eyes. "Thanks," she said.

"What song was that?" Joe asked. "It sounded kind of familiar."

Suddenly his face cleared, and he snapped his fingers. "I know! It's that new Buddy Death song. Boy, talk about different styles, though!"

He laughed out loud, not noticing that the girl's expression had grown cold. Abruptly she slung her guitar over her shoulder, turned, and stalked off.

"Hey! What'd I say?" Joe called, bewildered. The girl kept walking, her fists clenched and her back straight.

"Oh, well. Win some, lose some." With a shrug Joe let the door swing shut and headed back down the tunnel to find Frank and Callie. As he walked past Buddy Death's motor home he heard angry shouting.

Through a gap in the curtains covering a window Joe could see two men arguing. Joe recognized Buddy Death. He was tall and lanky with pale white skin and long, snarled black hair. The other man, a head shorter than Buddy, was slim, dark-haired, and deeply tanned.

Joe moved closer to the window. Though the men were yelling loudly, he couldn't make out any words.

Just then the door swung open and the short, dark man stormed out. He checked around, probably to see if anyone had heard the commotion, and then disappeared down tunnel C. Joe, who stood in the shadows behind the motor home, relaxed. The man hadn't seen him. Nor had he noticed the fat blue-jeaned roadie who had walked up behind Joe to watch the show.

"I wonder what that was about," Joe said to the roadie, whose grim expression was almost hidden behind a drooping mustache.

"Just Bobby and Buddy goin' at it as usual," the fat man drawled. "Bobby is Buddy's manager. They fight so much it's a wonder they get any work done." The roadie ambled off.

Nothing was happening there, so Joe continued toward the stage, where Callie, Frank, and Schacht had joined the other members of Buddy Death's band.

"There you are, Joe," said Callie as he joined them. "Just in time to meet the one and only Skeezer Bodine, Buddy's bass player." Joe shook hands with Skeezer, a small, elfin man with thinning blond hair. Then Callie introduced him to Sammy Shine, the drummer. Sammy was a rail-thin nineteen-year-old with a mop of bright red hair that hung down almost to his waist.

"Nice to meet you, man," Sammy said enthusiastically as he pumped Joe's hand. "And this here's our lead guitarist, Eric Holiday." Joe was reaching over to shake hands with the bearish guitar player when a loud bang startled everyone.

"Uh-oh," said Holiday.

Joe followed Holiday's gaze toward the black motor home. Buddy Death had kicked open the door and was stalking toward the stage. The heavy metal musician wore mirrored sunglasses, but still his expression wasn't hard to read. His mouth formed a tight, angry line.

He stomped up the stairs to the stage. "Syd!" he screamed. "Are we ready for lighting rehearsal or not?"

"Sure, Buddy." Schacht hurried over to

Buddy's side. "We were just waiting for our star."

"All right! Let's get this show on the road!" Buddy yelled.

Skeezer and the others immediately moved into place on several large Xs chalked on the stage.

Buddy strode up to center stage, then stood looking around in bewilderment. "Hey, where's my mike stand?" he demanded.

Schacht turned pale. "It won't be here till tonight. The sound truck had a flat."

"I need my stand, man!"

Schacht turned to the fat roadie Joe had talked to earlier. "Tex, dig up a mike stand."

Just then Joe heard a screech of metal overhead. He glanced up at the network of catwalks and supports that hung over the front of the stage. A giant spotlight suspended directly over Buddy's head had partially broken away from its support batten and was swinging by only one bolt. Joe made a dash up the steps and onto the stage.

"Watch out!" he yelled. But he was too late. The spotlight broke loose, falling straight for Buddy!

Chapter 2

BUDDY WAS ROOTED to his spot by fear, his mouth hanging open as he stared up at the plummeting spotlight.

Before Frank had time to react he saw a flash of movement from out of the corner of his eye.

It was Joe diving at lightning speed for Buddy.

A split second before the giant light reached Buddy, Joe had plowed into him at waist level, sending both of them flying several feet from the impact area.

The spotlight tore through the stage with a thunderous impact and finally came to rest on the mangled network of steel struts under the stage. One corner of it stuck up out of the stage floor at a crazy angle.

Everyone onstage clustered around Joe and Buddy. Frank and Callie started to help Joe up from where he lay sprawled.

"Are you okay, Joe?" Callie asked anxiously.

Joe didn't reply immediately, which worried Frank for a moment until Joe mimed that he was all right and had just had the wind knocked out of him.

Just then there was a frantic shout from the stands. Frank turned to see a skinny figure in a black motorcycle jacket waving his arms in the air.

"What's that kid doing here?" Schacht pulled a walkie-talkie from his back pocket. "Security! There's an unauthorized person in the arena! I want him apprehended and brought to me!"

Skeezer, who had helped Buddy to sit up, was anxiously asking him, "Buddy, you all right?"

Meanwhile Frank and Callie had helped Joe up, too.

"That was close!" Joe said shakily, running a hand through his hair.

"Yeah, too close!" Frank said as he picked up his camera. Using his camera's telephoto lens, he aimed it up at the bracket where the spotlight had hung. "They'd better have some pictures for the police."

While Frank was taking pictures a potbellied security guard dragged the struggling teenager in the motorcycle jacket up the stairs and onto the stage. The teenager had a scared expression on his pale, undernourished face. He struggled to escape the guard's grip.

"Here he is, Mr. Schacht," the guard announced. "I got the little weasel."

"Okay, kid, what are you doing here?" Schacht asked angrily.

"N-nothing," the skinny boy stammered. He tossed his mop of dark, greasy hair. "I just wanted to hear Buddy practice, I swear!"

"How'd you get past the security guards?" Joe asked curiously.

The potbellied guard frowned. "Why don't you butt out, sonny?" he growled at Joe. "Leave the interrogating to professionals."

"I didn't do anything!" the teenager squealed.

"Shut up, kid!" The guard jerked the boy's arm roughly for emphasis. "Let's see what's in your pockets."

A quick search turned up a set of motorcycle keys, six crumpled dollar bills, a package of chewing gum, an adjustable crescent wrench, and a small knife.

"This wrench could've loosened the bolts on the spotlight," Joe said.

The teen's eyes grew round. "Hey, wait a minute! I had nothing to do with that light. I was just watching Buddy. I wasn't anywhere near it, I swear!"

"Let the kid go." Sammy Shine spoke up from where he sat on an equipment case. "He couldn't have gotten up to or down from the catwalks without somebody seeing him."

"What's everybody waiting for? Call the cops!" Buddy demanded. "This guy tried to kill me!"

"Now, Buddy, let's not jump to any conclusions," Schacht said quickly. "We don't need that kind of publicity right at the start of the tour. What if it gives some nut the idea to do a copycat crime at a later gig?"

"Then arrest him for trespassing!"

"I don't think so." He turned to the frightened boy. "What's your name, son?"

"D-David Pauling, sir."

Schacht nodded and turned to the guard. "Take him back to security and question him. If he seems clean, let him go."

The guard's mouth fell open in astonishment, but he knew it was no use arguing. "Come back to my office, Pauling," he ordered, and he led the boy down the stairs and toward his office.

Joe went over to his brother, who had put the viewfinder of his camera to his eye and was searching the catwalks.

"Frank, don't you want to be there when they question that kid?" Joe asked impatiently.

"Nope," Frank replied. "This is none of our business, or had you forgotten?"

Suddenly Frank noticed a flicker of movement among the struts surrounding the fallen spotlight. With a twist of his wrist he changed the focus on the lens. A figure dressed in black from head to toe emerged from the background. The black-clad figure was down on one knee, and it appeared that he was tying something shiny onto one of the struts. As soon as he brought him into focus Frank snapped a picture. As the auto-rewind whirred and Frank pressed the shutter again the figure glanced down and noticed him. Instantly the black-clad person moved behind a cluster of pin spots and scuttled into the shadows.

"Hey! There's somebody up there!" Frank shouted as he snapped half a dozen more photos in rapid succession. He thrust his camera bag and camera at Callie.

"Frank, what—"

"No time to explain!" Frank sprinted to the ladder at stage left that led to the jungle of catwalks, cables, and spotlights above the stage. "Joe—go up the ladder stage right. See if we can trap that guy!" Frank called over his shoulder.

Frank leapt from the ladder to the nearest catwalk and moved along it as fast as he dared. By the time he reached the hole where the spotlight had been there was no sign of the stranger.

Frank checked down the catwalk that curved around the sides of the arena dome for any sign of movement. As far as Frank could tell it was empty, as were the catwalks that ran across the width of the dome and the one that stretched from the north end of the arena all the way to the south end.

He peered into the tangle of spotlights, cables, and supports over the stage but couldn't make out any movement there.

This is weird, Frank thought, edging out on the narrow catwalk toward the center of the dome. The guy vanished into thin air—

Frank's thoughts were cut short as he tripped and stumbled forward.

"Help!" Frank shouted as his feet fell out from under him. His arms windmilled frantically as he tried to grab on to anything for support. Just as he totally lost his balance one hand grabbed a guy wire that steadied the catwalk. Frank's body slipped off the catwalk, and the thin wire cut into his palm with searing pain. But he hung on grimly.

"Help! Somebody come quick!" Frank's body hung from the single wire. The arena's concrete floor was a full thirty feet below. "Help! I'm falling!"

Chapter 3

"HANG ON, FRANK!" Joe yelled, climbing onto Frank's catwalk and running toward his brother.

Just then Frank heard a shout from above. "Okay, kid—I've got you!"

Frank turned his head up as far as he dared and spotted a muscular, bearded man perched on the steel supports just under the top of the dome. To Frank's astonishment, the big roadie seemed to be falling toward him.

He jerked to a stop right beside Frank, suspended from a nylon safety line attached to his harness. He grabbed and held on to Frank, who noticed the roadie's many tattoos. His left shoulder bore the emblem of the navy's elite SEAL unit with a black dagger through it. His right forearm bore a blue lightning bolt.

Joe helped pull Frank onto the catwalk, then gave the big man a hand.

Frank also extended his hand to the roadie, then winced as the man's iron grip crushed his injured palm.

"Thanks, mist—" Frank began, his words turning to a yelp of pain.

"Forget it, kid," the roadie growled with a Brooklyn accent. "All in a day's work."

"I'm Frank Hardy, and this is my brother, Joe."

"I'm Kong," the roadie growled.

"You sure are," Joe joked, still shaken. "It sure was lucky you were close enough to help Frank."

The big man's expression grew stern. "If you're gonna be working up here, you wear safety harnesses! It's not safe to go stumbling around."

"I didn't stumble. I was tripped," Frank corrected him.

"What tripped you?" Joe cut in.

"I'm not sure, but it left a nasty welt on my shin."

"Here's what did it—piano wire!" Joe cried. He pointed to a piece of silver wire that lay flattened across the catwalk. "Looks like whoever you saw up here wasn't eager to be followed."

"What I want now is a closer look at the bracket that spotlight fell from," Frank said.

"Who are you guys, anyway? What were you doing up here?" Kong demanded, an angry edge to his voice.

Ignoring him, Frank moved carefully out to the bracket so he could examine it closely.

"I knew it!" he said triumphantly. Four bolts dangled loosely from the back of the bracket. Frank examined them for wear and saw that they were all new and shiny. There was no sign of breakage or torn metal.

"That spotlight didn't tear loose," Frank called over to his brother. "It was deliberately dropped."

"Are you sure?" Joe asked as Frank made his way back to Joe's catwalk.

"Positive. The heads of the bolts aren't even scarred, so whatever did it had the right kind of tools for the job."

"Man, Frank, you are one lucky guy that Kong was right there." Joe led the way back to the ladder. Kong, scowling, followed a short distance behind.

"Maybe it wasn't just luck that he happened to be there," Frank muttered as soon as Kong was out of hearing range.

"What do you mean?" Joe muttered back.

"That piano wire was a professional booby trap, Joe. And I just noticed Kong had a tattoo from the navy's SEALs, their guerrilla outfit."

"You think Kong—"

"I don't want to talk about it right now," Frank whispered, glancing behind them at Kong.

As soon as the brothers hit the stage Callie ran to Frank and wrapped her arms around him. "You scared me to death," she said. "Don't ever do that again!"

Frank started to reply, but just then he heard a shout from the far end of the arena. "Syd!" yelled a tall, dark-haired, barrel-chested man dressed in denim overalls and a tie-dyed shirt. He hurried toward the stage, waving a sheet of paper. His blue eyes shone with grim urgency under dark, bushy eyebrows.

"Where were you, Jake?" Kong boomed at him. "Somebody tried to squash His Majesty with a spotlight."

"Huh? What're you talking about?" Jake stopped in confusion.

"A spotlight came loose over the stage. It almost crushed Buddy," Schacht told him.

"And when I went up to investigate," Frank added, "I fell over a trip wire the joker left behind. It almost killed me."

"Who are you?" Jake asked Frank belligerently.

"Take it easy, Jake," Schacht said in a low voice. "These kids are Frank and Joe

Hardy. They came in with a reporter." Schacht turned to the Hardys. "Boys, this is Jake Williams, my road boss and special effects supervisor. Now, what's that paper you're waving around, Jake?"

Jake handed it to him without a word. While Schacht scanned it Joe looked over his shoulder. The note was printed in pencil in block letters.

> Buddy Death is too evil to live. He will not perform in Bayport or anywhere else, for he'll soon be dead.
>
> Blade

"Where did you find this?" Joe asked.

Jake looked at him quizzically, then replied, "It was pinned on the door of the office that Schacht's using with this." He produced a slim, deadly looking dagger from the side pocket of his overalls.

"Looks like a standard-issue U.S. combat knife," Frank said. "They give them to the army and marines, but the prankster could have bought one at a surplus store."

Schacht looked at the Hardys with increased interest. "Jake, will you excuse us a minute?" he said.

He led Frank and Joe to the rear of the stage and made sure they were alone before speaking.

"What's going—" Joe began before Schacht cut him off impatiently.

"I just had a brainstorm," he explained. "I'm worried about what's going on here, but if it gets into the papers that there's some killer after Buddy, this concert's going to be dead for sure. I've got to stop this guy, but I can't afford to call in the cops."

He hesitated. "How'd you kids like to help Buddy and me out?" he said. "Sniff around, see what you come up with. I can give you jobs in the crew as cover."

Joe looked at his brother and grinned. "You don't have to ask us twice," he said eagerly.

"Great." Schacht seemed to be a little relieved.

"Where do you want us to start?" Frank asked.

"How about with your girlfriend?" Schacht indicated Callie, who stood talking with Eric, Sammy, and Skeezer. "She's got to keep quiet about this if we want to nab the guy."

"Mr. Schacht, if you're asking me to put a gag order on Callie's story, the answer is no," Frank replied firmly.

"Who said anything about a gag order?" Schacht replied. "I just want her to hold off on filing the story about the spotlight until you catch Blade."

"I don't know," said Frank.

"Look," Schacht offered, "I'll make you a

deal. You get her to wait twenty-four hours, and I'll make sure it's exclusive."

Frank frowned. "If it means that much to you, I'll give it my best shot. But no guarantees."

As Frank walked out of the wings Schacht told Joe Kong's legal name. Joe looked up and noticed that Jake Williams and Kong were standing to one side of the stage, watching them.

"Uh, there's Callie. You coming, Joe?" asked Frank.

"No way!" Joe shook his head. "Sweet-talking Callie is your department."

Joe watched with amusement as Frank led Callie away from Eric, Skeezer, and Sammy. Callie's smile faded as she listened to what Frank had to say, and the stubborn expression Joe knew so well appeared in its place.

"Oh, well. It's not my problem," he told himself, wandering toward the back of the stage. Schacht, too, hurried away, and the roadies went back to work. Joe wondered where the musicians had gone. He guessed the light rehearsal had been postponed until after the spotlight was replaced.

Just then Joe heard Buddy's voice from somewhere backstage. He peered into the darkness and finally spotted Buddy standing in the shadow of some wooden crates, talking heatedly with someone he couldn't see. Joe moved in closer to listen in on the rock star's conversation.

"I told you over and over again—I don't want you around, Clare! Are you stupid or what?"

"How can you be so mean to me after what we've been through?" said a tearful female voice.

"It's over, Clare. Just accept it and move on like I have," Buddy shouted.

Joe moved back into the shadows as Buddy turned and started stalking away from the unseen woman. Then he heard the woman begin to sob behind the crates.

Instinctively Joe moved toward her. As he did he stepped on a thin piece of wood that broke with a loud crack. Buddy froze in the wings, turned, and glared at Joe. Then without a word he marched off.

Joe immediately rounded the corner of the crate and saw the auburn-haired girl he'd met earlier. She stared up at him, wiping her eyes, and frowned.

"Hi," Joe said nervously. "Listen, I'm sorry if I offended you this afternoon." He took a step toward her.

"It's all right." She looked him in the eye for the first time. "You didn't know any better. Music is just a touchy subject with me." She pulled out a tissue and blew her nose.

"My name's Joe Hardy. I just joined the road crew." Joe stuck out his hand.

The girl smiled and shook Joe's hand briefly. "I'm Clare. Clare Williams. My brother Jake's the road boss for Buddy's group."

"Yeah, I met him," Joe said. "Listen, I couldn't help overhearing you just now," he went on. "Buddy was pretty rough on you."

Clare's smile disappeared instantly, and the angry, sullen scowl Joe had seen before reappeared. "What do you know about it?" she snapped. "Why don't you just mind your own business?"

"I was just trying to help," said Joe.

"Nosy's more like it. If I need your help, I'll ask for it!" Furious, Clare pushed past a stunned Joe Hardy and ran off into the darkness.

"Okay already!" Joe stared after her and shook his head. "Boy, that girl sure is touchy."

He wandered back onstage and found Frank and Callie both smiling. Frank must have offered to keep Callie posted on the progress of their investigation, he realized. Callie enjoyed a good mystery almost as much as a great scoop.

"Hi," Joe called as he approached them. "Everything work out all right?"

Frank nodded. "We—came to an understanding."

Suddenly they heard someone shouting from

the other end of the stage. Joe turned to see Buddy pointing at him.

"Hey, punk!" Buddy yelled. "What're you doing on my stage? I saw you spying on me, you little creep!" He marched over to Joe, his green eyes flashing dangerously. The nearby crew members backed away out of danger.

"I wasn't spying on you. I just happened to be walking by when you were yelling at that poor girl," Joe said evenly.

"You shut up!" Buddy screamed. He was shaking with fear and anger. "I want you out of here, or there's going to be trouble!" He pushed Joe in the chest.

"Stop it," Joe said quietly, anger flashing in his eyes.

"Take it easy, man," he heard Frank say. "What's the matter with you?"

"I want both of you out of here!" Buddy shouted. Snarling with rage, he reached for a nearby pile of scrap lumber and grabbed a two-by-four. Brandishing it like a baseball bat, he advanced on the Hardys.

"What are you doing?" Callie screamed. "Watch out, Joe! He's going to kill you!"

Chapter 4

JOE DUCKED as Buddy swung the two-by-four. Frank saw it miss his head by a fraction of an inch. He dived onto the stage and rolled to his left, coming up in a fighting crouch several steps from Buddy.

Seeing that Joe was out of reach, Buddy turned on Frank and ran toward him, swinging the plank.

"Callie—get out of here!" Frank yelled.

As Buddy swung the board Frank grabbed the end of it with both hands, yanking it from Buddy's grasp.

Buddy stumbled past Frank, then turned and charged him again.

Frank agilely sidestepped Buddy's charge and tripped him, sending him sprawling.

"What's going on here?" Schacht shouted angrily as he ran across the stage.

"Your star tried to crown us," Joe said, barely containing his temper.

"Take it easy, Buddy. What's the problem here?" Schacht asked soothingly.

"I don't want strangers hanging around here, Syd! I told you that!" Buddy yelled.

"They aren't strangers. I hired them for your road crew."

Buddy glared at Frank and Joe. "How do I know one of them's not Blade?" he demanded.

"Buddy, baby, I promise. Joe saved your life just a few minutes ago. Why would he rig a light to fall and then risk his neck saving you? Also I know their dad personally! We'll get Blade, but he ain't going to be one of these two."

At these words Buddy calmed down, but he still scowled doubtfully at the brothers. "It better not be," he grumbled at last. "I don't like strangers around me, Syd, You keep these guys out of my hair!"

Frank watched Buddy stalk off. "All right, I accept your apology," he quipped. Joe added, "Thanks for the thank-you for saving your life."

"The kid's on edge," Schacht tried to explain. "Heavy metal bands have been taking enough flak in the media already. Now he's got to worry about people staying away from his concerts because they think they're unsafe. Not to mention the question of his own survival."

"Yeah, okay," Joe said impatiently. "Just give us a place to start with this."

Schacht motioned for Frank and Joe to come nearer. "Work closely with the roadies," he whispered. "See what the word of mouth is on this Blade character."

"Was today the first time anything like this has happened?" Frank asked.

Schacht hesitated. Then he shrugged. "Okay, you might as well know everything," he said. "We got another note two days ago. Same block printing, same signature."

"Why didn't you tell us this before?" Joe wanted to know.

"Bobby Mellor and I agreed not to talk about it. We figured it was just a crank letter. Buddy's already nervous enough about this tour. We've got the note back at our hotel."

"Does Buddy get a lot of crank letters?" Frank asked.

"A few. Mostly they're from parents who don't like his music. Blade's letters were the only serious threats."

"We'll need to do some background checks on the people around Buddy right away," Frank decided.

Schacht nodded. "Okay. I'll tell Jake and

Bobby that you're running errands for me. How's that?"

"Good," Joe replied. "This shouldn't take more than a few hours."

After returning to the Hardy home Frank, Joe, and Callie held a quick planning session in the kitchen.

"Since I've already dug up some info on Buddy, I can finish snooping into his past," Callie volunteered.

"Good." Frank smiled at her. "See if you can find evidence that Buddy was threatened before."

"While she's doing that, Frank, I'll dig around for info on Bobby Mellor and the guys on the crew," Joe suggested.

"Good," Frank agreed. "I'll see what I can come up with from that law enforcement data net Dad uses."

As soon as Callie left to go to the library to read old newspapers and Joe went to work in Fenton Hardy's office, Frank began searching the law enforcement data bank on his computer, using his father's access code. Soon Kong's complete military history appeared on the screen. "Wow," Frank said, scrolling down the list of information. Not only had Kong spent five years in the navy, two of them in the elite SEAL commando unit, but he also had a lengthy criminal record since being dishonorably discharged from the navy.

"All right. A lead at last," Frank said to himself. He instructed his computer to print up a hard copy of Kong's military record and rap sheet and then moved on to the other suspects.

Hours later a rumble in Frank's stomach reminded him how many hours had passed since breakfast. He went downstairs to the kitchen and found Joe already there, munching on their Aunt Gertrude's chocolate-chip cookies.

"Just in time," Joe said as Frank seated himself across the table and snagged a handful of cookies. "I found something interesting in Mellor's credit records."

"Don't tell me, let me guess," Frank replied with a smile. "All his credit records go back only five years. So do all his other records, according to the data net."

"What do you make of that?" Joe asked.

"I'd say we have two choices—he's in a witness protection program or he's hiding out from creditors or something. I also checked out that crazy fan, David Pauling. His rap sheet consists of one traffic ticket. The address he gave the police officer is a vacant lot in the waterfront district. And there's more," Frank added.

Just then Callie appeared at the kitchen

door, and Frank stopped talking to open the door for her.

"Hi, guys," she said. "Not much hot stuff on Buddy, but I photocopied everything, anyway. I thought if we went over it together, you might turn up something I missed. What did you get?" she asked Frank.

"I was just about to tell Joe that both Jake and Kong were in the service," Frank said, handing Callie a cookie. "Jake was in the Army Corps of Engineers until about five years ago, specializing in demolition. Kong was in the navy, and both guys were stationed in Japan at the same time."

"Maybe that's where they met," Callie speculated.

Frank nodded his head. "Now, here's the really interesting part, folks. Kong was in the elite navy SEAL unit. He was in the brig several times in the service and finally got booted out of the SEALs. He's been in and out of jail since he got out of the navy."

"For what?" Joe asked.

"He had multiple raps for assault, illegal weapons possession, one for illegal possession of dynamite, and two for burglary." Frank sat back with a satisfied expression.

Concern showed in Callie's face. "I want you to be careful around Kong. I don't trust him."

"Don't worry, Callie. We'll be careful around

everybody until we know for sure who Blade is."

"We should probably head back to the arena," Joe said, "before our absence looks suspicious."

As soon as they entered the arena Frank saw the security guard who had taken Pauling away striding toward the stage.

"Excuse me, Mr. Schacht," the guard said loudly. "I want to make my report before I go home."

Schacht waved the man over. "Sure. I want you to meet the newest members of my security team," he added in a low voice. "They're working undercover. Boys, this is Captain Hubbard."

Hubbard looked surprised and not very pleased at the news, but he shook hands with the boys, aware that Syd Schacht was watching.

"Now," said Schacht, "what did you learn from that kid in the motorcycle jacket?"

Hubbard squared his shoulders and began giving his report in a crisp voice. "His name's David Pauling. He's sixteen, a high school dropout, and unemployed. He's a big heavy metal fan, and if you ask me, he's obsessed with Buddy Death."

Schacht frowned. "You think he had anything to do with that spotlight falling?"

Before Hubbard could answer, Joe jumped in.

"We examined that spotlight bracket right after the light fell. The bolts looked like they were deliberately loosened. Pauling would have had to move pretty fast to loosen the bolts and then be down on the arena floor when it crashed."

Hubbard looked annoyed at the interruption, but Schacht seemed pleased at Joe's analysis.

"Anyway," Hubbard continued, "I let him go. I don't think he's dangerous, and I couldn't hold him for the knife he had on him because he has a clean record with the Bayport police."

"Would you mind giving us a look at your notes on Pauling so we can do a follow-up?" Frank asked.

Hubbard seemed reluctant, but Schacht prodded him.

"All right," Hubbard said. "Come back to my office."

As Hubbard turned to leave Kong came lumbering into view from the rear of the stage. "Sound truck's here, Mr. Schacht," he reported. Then, turning to Frank and Joe, he said, "Jake wants you down at the tunnel entrance ASAP, Hardys."

"We'll be there in a few minutes," said Frank.

"Jake wants you there now," Kong insisted.

"But—" Joe objected, and Kong planted himself menacingly in Joe's path.

"Don't worry, boys," Schacht said with a wink. "I'll take care of your errand myself."

"Let's go, Joe," Frank said to his brother. "No point in stirring up any more trouble."

Joe gave Kong a hard look before he followed his brother toward the stairs.

"Go through tunnel A," Kong instructed. "Jake's got everyone unloading so the sound crew can set up tonight."

"Tonight?" Frank said in surprise.

"What's the matter, you wimps afraid you'll miss your bedtime?" Kong taunted.

"Listen, mister, my brother and I can keep up with anybody on your road crew, including you," Joe retorted, his temper flaring.

Kong laughed. It was not a nice laugh.

"We'll see about that," he said.

A few minutes later sweat was pouring down Frank's face as he and Joe pushed big wheeled cases down a ramp from a semitrailer parked outside the arena at the mouth of access tunnel A. Jake stood near the bottom of the ramp with a clipboard, directing the roadies, while Kong supervised the unpacking of the cases with Manny Sterns, the head of the sound crew.

It seemed to Frank that he, Joe, and the other roadies had been unloading for hours without making a dent in the pile of equipment.

While they were working Frank saw Bobby Mellor arrive. He heard the manager ask Kong and Jake to climb into the equipment trailer, saying, "I need you to help me go over these equipment manifests."

Joe had stopped working to get a drink from a nearby water cooler.

"Quitting already, huh, punk?" Kong growled behind him.

"No. I just stopped for a drink of water, if that's okay with you, 'boss,' " Joe said sarcastically.

"Okay, you got your drink. Get back to work. There's still lots to do."

Frank saw what had happened and went over to his brother. "Take it easy, Joe. Let's just concentrate on the case."

As the Hardys started unloading equipment at the base of the ramp Frank heard a low rumbling sound. Instinctively he turned his head toward the noise. A dark shape was hurtling down the equipment ramp.

Frank glanced over his shoulder and saw that Joe was bending over a small crate, his back to the ramp. He seemed oblivious to the massive equipment case that was only seconds away from crushing him!

Chapter 5

"JOE!" FRANK SHOUTED.

Joe whipped around to see the case hurtling toward him. He threw himself backward. Beside him the big case roared down the ramp and smashed into Joe's crate, splintering it on impact.

"Joe, are you all right?" Frank peered anxiously into his brother's face.

"I'm okay, I guess," he replied, wincing as he got to his feet. "It's just my back. And my elbows. And my tailbone."

"What's going on out there?" an angry voice yelled from inside the truck. Joe and Frank turned to see Bobby Mellor striding over to the crate that the equipment case had smashed. Mellor's face was dark with anger.

"Five hundred bucks worth of equipment!" Mellor screamed, pointing at Joe. "You were unloading the stuff! It's your fault!"

"Hey, wait a second," Joe said angrily. "I didn't even touch the case!"

"Kong!" Mellor shouted. "Jake!"

Kong appeared in the doorway of the trailer and trotted over to where Mellor stood.

"These two morons smashed up a whole box of equipment! Get rid of them! Now!" he shouted, pointing at Frank and Joe.

Jake Williams suddenly jumped down from the trailer. "Let's all take it easy," he said quietly.

The group turned to look at the barrel-chested road manager. "Good idea," Frank agreed. "Look, we were just standing at the bottom of the ramp, and it came rolling down on us!"

"Okay," Mellor said, disgusted. "We've already wasted too much time. I want all this stuff in place for a sound and light check by midnight."

"All right, you heard the man," Jake shouted at the roadies who had crowded around the splintered crate. "Let's get on it, people! Frank, find Manny and ask what you can help with. Joe, you stay here with the rest of the crew."

Before Frank left, Joe pulled him aside for a quick conference. "That was no accident,

Frank. Could Blade already be on to us?" he asked in a low voice.

"Who knows?" Frank commented, adding, "But it's funny how Mellor appeared just before you nearly got flattened."

"I'll keep an eye on him," Joe replied.

"We shouldn't forget Kong and Jake were in there, too," Frank said. "Maybe one of them pushed it."

"The only thing we know for sure is that we can't rule anybody out," Joe replied.

The rest of the unloading went smoothly. When the semi was empty Joe helped to move the enormous speakers into the arena on wheeled carts. He watched as the speakers were hoisted up into the air by a small crane and bolted to the sound towers and the framework above the stage.

To Joe's surprise, it was only nine o'clock when he was told he could go home. He found Frank up in the catwalks helping Manny Sterns, a plump, pony-tailed man, to secure one of the speakers to a support. Joe pitched in, and the speaker was soon tightly bolted to its bracket.

"How much longer do you think you'll be working?" Joe asked his brother.

"That's up to Manny here."

"You can go," Manny told him. "Just be back here at six tomorrow morning."

"See you then," Frank said. He and Joe

climbed down from the catwalk and headed for the arena's parking lot.

Joe yawned as he and Frank walked up to their van. "Boy, I'm beat," he confessed. "I never realized being a roadie was such hard work."

"I have some more work to do before we turn in tonight," Frank replied. "I want to develop those photos I took."

Joe glanced at his watch. "Speedy Photo closed a few minutes ago."

"Ah, but I have a secret weapon," Frank said with a crafty smile. "Duke Wampler from my calculus class works there, and he owes me a favor. Let's hope he stayed late. I'll drop you off at Mr. Pizza. Order us a large pie with the works. I'll meet you there in twenty minutes."

Joe noticed his brother's disappointed expression the minute Frank appeared in Mr. Pizza. He quickly understood why after scanning the prints. They were hopelessly blurred, showing just the back of an indistinct figure in black on the catwalks above the stage. Even magnified, the photos were only slightly clearer.

"This is it?" Joe asked in disbelief.

Frank nodded. "Yep. That last picture is the best Duke could do with the enlarger. It shows where the guy's shirt had pulled out of his pants. See, there's some kind of intricate design on his T-shirt underneath."

"Where does that leave us?" Joe asked.

"Back at square one, I guess." Frank reached for a slice of pizza.

"Then let's eat this pie and get out of here." Joe shoved the photos back into the envelope. "We have to be up at the crack of dawn tomorrow."

When Joe awoke the next morning he found Frank standing over him already dressed.

"Hurry up, Joe. We only have half an hour to get to the arena."

"What about breakfast?" Joe mumbled.

"Jake said they always feed the crews on these arena jobs."

Joe nodded sleepily and reached for the jeans draped over the chair next to his bed. "I knew there had to be *some* reason people took this job," he said.

When they walked into the arena Joe saw that most of the roadies were already there, clustered around tables set up on the arena floor beside the stage. The tables were laden with pastries, fruit, cereal, bacon, and scrambled eggs.

At the sight of food Joe felt himself perking up. His stomach rumbled as he made a beeline for the trays of pastries. After loading his plate with sweet rolls and doughnuts Joe searched for Frank and saw him sitting with some of the sound crew, a plate full of fruit balanced on his lap.

The one thing that still puzzled Joe was why anyone would want to kill Buddy Death. Now, he figured, was as good a time as any to see what he could find out about the rock star from the people who worked for him.

Spotting the fat, mustached roadie named Tex sitting on a crate, Joe went over and joined him.

"Hi," Joe said. "Mind if I sit here?"

"Naw, go ahead," Tex twanged.

"Thanks," Joe replied. "Sure is nice to have a hot breakfast, huh?"

"Yeah," Tex agreed. "We're going to need it with the day we got ahead of us."

"They sure work us hard," Joe commented.

"Well, I don't mind working hard, but I wish we were working for some other band, man."

"Why's that?" Joe asked. "Don't you like working for Buddy?"

"Nope," Tex replied. "I think he's a jerk."

"Why?" Joe inquired.

"Because he hassles his road crew. But I guess a no-talent punk like Buddy doesn't know any better. He's made a lot of enemies already."

"Oh, yeah? Like who?"

"Like Kong, for instance," Tex said, sipping his coffee. " 'Course, Kong's been ticked off at Buddy for years. Even before working on this tour."

"How come?" Joe asked in surprise.

" 'Cause of Clare Williams. She and Buddy were a real item a few years back. But when Buddy started heading for the big time he dumped her. She was never the same after that."

"Hmm," Joe said thoughtfully. Now there was some information that might turn into a good lead, he thought. "But what's that got to do with Kong?"

Tex just shook his head. "Kong and Jake, Clare's brother, are old friends from way back. Kong always thought the sun rose and set on Clare. When Buddy dumped her Kong got really mad."

"Interesting," Joe muttered to himself. He excused himself and casually sauntered over to Frank. "Hey, Frank," Joe said quietly, "can we talk?"

Frank looked up and grinned at him. "You read my mind, Joe. Let's go somewhere we can talk privately."

Joe led his brother over behind a stack of empty packing boxes, where they were out of sight from the rest of the crew.

"You've got that look in your eye, Joe. What'd you pick up?" Frank said eagerly.

"A motive, maybe. Did you know Kong hates Buddy's guts?"

Frank nodded. "Yeah. Some of the guys were telling me all about how Buddy dumped Jake's sister. And that she's been following the tour around ever since."

"But if it's Jake's sister who got dumped, what's Jake's attitude?" Joe wondered.

Frank looked thoughtful. "Jake doesn't seem to care. He hired on to do this tour after Buddy dumped Clare, and the roadies say all he's ever done is tell Clare to go home."

"What about Bobby Mellor?" Joe put in. "I saw him having a major screaming match with Buddy in his motor home. And I still want to know what he was doing *six* years ago."

Frank started to reply but was interrupted by the sudden arrival of Buddy's limo through access tunnel B. It screeched to a stop near the food tables, startling several roadies into dropping their plates.

"Why's he here so early?" Joe asked Frank.

"I heard he's an early-morning nut," Frank answered.

"All right, breakfast's over! Time to get to work!" Buddy announced as his limo door flew open.

Kong separated himself from one group and

went over to stand in front of Buddy, glowering at him.

"We go to work when Jake tells us to, not you," Kong growled.

"I don't want any of your lip, ugly," Buddy told him. "I'm the star here. I could have you fired any time."

"Oh, yeah? You fire me, and Jake and half the crew'll walk. And then where will you be, Mr. High-and-Mighty Rock Star?" Kong shouted, taking a step toward Buddy.

Joe saw Buddy flinch, then stand his ground.

"You're crazy if you think I'm afraid of you, you big goon," Buddy said, turning a shade paler than usual.

But before the confrontation went any further Jake and Bobby Mellor emerged from the nearest access tunnel.

"Okay, breakfast's over. Let's get it on, people!" Jake bellowed. "How about a little hustle, gang? There's a big press conference tonight, and I want all the special effects ready to go."

Joe drained his juice, and then he and Frank went over to Jake, who was reading the roadies' assignments off a clipboard. Frank was again assigned to work with the sound crew, while Jake told Joe to get a safety harness from Kong and gave him his assignment. "Joe, I want you to climb the right sound tower and make sure all the speakers are hooked up. Start at the top and work your way down. Ordinarily I'd have one of the sound crew check it, but they're spread pretty thin today."

"You got it," Joe replied. Then he went to find Kong. Kong gave Joe the tools he'd need and a nylon harness.

Joe then went over to the tower and began climbing. The scaffolding was easy to scale, but it creaked ominously as Joe went higher. As he neared the top the tower began swaying. This gives me the creeps, Joe said to himself, but when he looked down he saw Kong watching his progress. He thinks I'm going to wimp out, Joe thought angrily. His anger made him move up the stack faster.

As Joe kept climbing the swaying of the tower grew more pronounced. When he reached the top he hooked his safety line to a beam just above the topmost cluster of speakers.

The swaying motion, which had seemed gentle at first, had become a violent swinging from side to side. Joe's right foot slipped from the crossbeam on which he was standing. He scrambled desperately for a hold.

He heard a loud, high-pitched screeching of bending metal, and then the tower shuddered forward.

Joe clung to the corner as the tower fell, thinking about the thousands of pounds of steel that seemed determined to crush him.

Chapter 6

"LOOK OUT! THE TOWER'S FALLING!" Frank shrieked from the overhead catwalk as the sound tower pitched forward with Joe hooked to its underside. *Joe will be crushed,* he thought, frustrated by his own helplessness.

Then, at the very last moment, Joe unhooked his safety line and leapt free of the tower. His arms and legs windmilled frantically as he lunged out for the edge of the fabric canopy that was stretched over the apron and the front half of the stage.

When he saw Joe catch the edge of the canopy Frank felt himself breathe again.

The sound tower crashed to the arena floor a second later with a *clonk* of hollow metal on concrete, just missing the edge of the stage.

Bent support struts and crossbeams flew in all directions, causing roadies to dive behind any available cover.

Frank barely noticed these things as he scrambled along the catwalk. Below him, at stage right, Frank saw with vast relief that Tex and Benny, another roadie who had been working in the lighting grid over the stage, were pulling Joe up from the edge of the canopy.

"Joe, are you hurt?" Tex asked as he pulled him onto the catwalk.

"I'm all right," Joe replied.

Frank saw that his brother was descending the stage-right ladder.

"That was a close one," Frank said after descending a ladder and meeting his brother on the stage.

"Courtesy of our pal Blade, I bet," said Joe.

"That tower falling did seem a little too convenient to be an accident," Frank agreed.

"Let's have a look at it," said Joe.

Frank jumped down from the edge of the stage to examine the twisted struts from the tower as Buddy emerged from his motor home. He kicked the side door open with a bang.

"Now what's gone wrong?" he shouted as he stomped toward the wreckage of the sound tower.

Benny told Buddy what had happened, pointing at Joe as he told him. Buddy fixed Joe with a look of rage and strode over to him.

"Man, everything you touch you destroy!" Buddy yelled at Joe. "My stage may not be ready for tonight's press conference! You're history! Finito!"

"Joe was on top of the tower and was lucky to get down in one piece. He didn't have anything to do with it falling down. Maybe you should try to find out why that tower fell before you have them clear away the wreckage," Frank suggested.

Mellor looked at Frank with an impatient expression, then snapped, "I don't care why it's down. I just want to see it up again. And fast!"

That's a funny attitude to take, Frank thought.

Roadies moved in from every corner of the arena to start picking up the pieces. Joe held them off for a few minutes while he examined the wreckage of the tower.

"You sound like you don't care whether or not Blade gets Buddy," Frank ventured.

Mellor gave him a speculative look before answering.

"Sometimes I wish I'd never found that creep. When I discovered Buddy he was fronting for some nothing bar band in New York City. I recognized his potential and created his image. You'd think he'd be grateful, but not him!" Mellor's voice rose to a high pitch, and Frank noticed that his face was turning a deep shade of red.

Mellor sighed heavily and then seemed to get control of himself. With a shake of his head he smoothed his hair back. "Sorry if I went off there for a second. It's just hard for me, knowing that as soon as I help make Buddy a star he's going to tear up his management contract with me and split."

"You sound pretty certain of that," Frank observed.

"Are you kidding me?" Mellor said bitterly. "That creep has stabbed every friend he ever had in the back. All he cares about is making it to the top of the rock biz. As soon as he thinks he's used me up, I'm history."

Abruptly, as if sensing he'd said too much, Mellor ended his conversation and turned away.

"Better get to work. I've got a lot to do," he muttered as he walked out.

Frank looked at the tower wreckage on the arena floor and saw Joe beckoning him to come over.

"What did you find, Joe?" he asked.

Joe held up a metal standard, one of the corner supports that the horizontal cross-beams and diagonal support struts were bolted to.

Puzzled, Frank examined it but didn't see what was wrong with it. "I don't get it, Joe," he said, handing it back.

"It looks like somebody deliberately sabotaged it by removing the locking pins from the corner support," Joe told him, pointing at the empty slots where the cotter pins went.

"Maybe the pins got dislodged when the tower fell."

Joe shook his head. "Not likely. I examined all the other standards. The locking pins were bent, but they were all in place," he said firmly.

Over Joe's shoulder Frank spotted Jake Williams trotting out of access tunnel A. Jake looked sweaty and anxious as he surveyed the wreckage.

"Oh, great! Another disaster! I better order the steel for another tower now if we're going to be ready for the rehearsal," Jake muttered as he trotted down the tunnel he'd come out of.

"This has got to be Blade's work, but who is Blade?" Joe asked.

Frank shrugged his shoulders. "It could be Mellor, or Kong, or even Jake. Blade has to be working from the inside. One of the roadies or even you and I would have noticed a stranger moving around here. What do you think?"

"I don't know why," Joe told him, "but

I've got a gut feeling that Mellor might be Blade. He looked mad enough to kill when he was talking to me about Buddy."

"That doesn't make sense, Joe. I don't think Mellor would knock off the man who was his bread and butter."

"Mellor doesn't strike me as the most stable guy in the world," Joe insisted stubbornly. "He may be so eaten up with resentment that he's not thinking rationally. Besides, think about this: Mellor's been right there every time Blade caused an accident."

"There were a lot of people around after the accidents. Kong and Jake were usually around, too," Frank retorted.

"But think about it, Frank. Mellor was the only one around after all three accidents Blade arranged. And there is still the question of all those missing years."

Frank paused and reflected on what Joe was saying and had to admit that he was right. But a little voice in the back of his head told him not to jump to any hasty conclusions.

"Come on, Joe, you know we have to have solid evidence before we can make any accusations. We don't have anything at all like that. Besides, Kong and Jake still seem to have stronger motives because of Jake's sister."

"Well, all we can do is keep on digging," Joe replied.

As Joe stood up the other roadies began

clearing away the sound tower and loading it on wheeled carts that Kong and Tex had pushed up beside the wreckage.

Looking up from his work a couple of hours later, Frank saw Schacht emerge from Buddy's motor home and mop his brow with a brightly colored handkerchief.

"How'd it go with Buddy, Mr. Schacht?" Joe asked as Schacht walked past the roadies up to the stage.

Schacht shook his head. "One of these days I'm going to smack that little weasel right in the kisser," he said. "But at least I got him calmed down enough to rehearse."

"Where's the rest of the band?" Frank asked.

"They travel in a separate limo," Schacht replied. "Speaking of which, where are those guys?"

"Here we are, Syd," Skeezer Bodine called cheerfully from the wings. "We came in the back way."

Turning, Frank saw Skeezer, Sammy, and Eric amble onstage, talking and laughing. Sammy wore a wild yellow suede outfit with fringe on the legs and arms, while Skeezer and Eric wore T-shirts and torn jeans. Kong and two other roadies followed them and set up microphone stands, Sammy's elaborate drum kit with a big bass drum bearing the Buddy Death Band logo, a V-shaped array of electronic drums, his cymbals and a rack of congas, and assorted percussion instruments. It took Kong only a few minutes to put up Buddy's mike stand and lay out Eric's guitars and Skeezer's electric bass, all bearing the black and white BDB logo.

Despite all the accidents that had plagued the gig so far, Frank thought the band members were in good spirits, especially Sammy and Skeezer. Skeezer had taken his electric bass from its stand and was doing a duckwalk across the stage while making funny faces at Sammy and Eric.

"And that's how Chuck Berry does it," Frank heard Skeezer say.

Sammy slapped the tops of his thighs and laughed hard. "That's great, man! Who else can you do?"

Skeezer looked at Sammy slyly from under his pale blond eyebrows. "I do a wicked Buddy Death imitation," he said modestly.

"Do it, Skeezer," Sammy insisted. "Come on, man. We could all use a good laugh."

Skeezer smiled and shook his head. "No, I better not. What if His Highness sees me? We could all be in the soup then."

"Oh, go ahead, Skeezer," Eric prodded.

"Okay, okay," Skeezer said, taking off his bass and handing it to Joe. He took a moment to compose himself, then threw out his chest and began strutting around the stage pretending to sing into a microphone.

"I am the greatest rock star of all time!" Skeezer howled in a hilariously accurate parody of Buddy's voice.

Frank smiled and heard the other band members and roadies laughing. Frank had seen Buddy perform only in music videos, but he had to admit Skeezer had Buddy's mannerisms down perfectly.

Skeezer strutted from one side of the stage to the other until the roadies were howling with laughter. Frank noticed Sammy lying on his back, laughing so hard his legs were kicking in the air.

Wearing a near-perfect copy of the sneer Buddy wore on the cover of his first album, Skeezer strode over to Buddy's mike stand and grabbed it. As soon as he touched the mike stand his eyes got wide and his body went rigid. Frank immediately knew something was wrong. Skeezer began shaking as if he were having a fit. Frank heard sizzling sounds and smelled a sharp tang of ozone.

Frank heard the laughter end abruptly as everyone realized that Skeezer was being electrocuted!

Chapter 7

IN A FLASH Frank scooped up a wooden broom and flicked the long end of the broom handle, knocking the mike stand away from Skeezer.

As soon as Frank broke contact between Skeezer's hands and the mike stand Skeezer collapsed on the stage and lay there twitching. Frank threw down the broom handle and bent over Skeezer, ready to administer CPR if Skeezer needed it.

Everyone crowded up onstage, roadies and rockers alike, and they all surged forward to see if Skeezer was all right.

Joe flicked a glance over at Schacht and saw the promoter mopping his face with his handkerchief and talking to himself.

"Not Skeezer," Schacht muttered. "As if I didn't have enough disasters on my hands already."

Schacht suddenly turned to Tex and shouted, "Where's Jake? Where's Bobby? Is somebody calling an ambulance?"

Realizing that nobody else had had the presence of mind to do so, Joe ran toward a pay phone he remembered seeing near the mouth of tunnel A. He dialed 911 and requested an ambulance.

When Joe returned he saw, to his relief, that Skeezer was sitting up, supported by Frank.

Joe pushed through the people standing around Frank and Skeezer. "How is he, Frank?"

Frank looked up, his face serious, and replied, "He's had a bad jolt and has some burns on his hands, but I think he'll be all right."

Sammy knelt down and patted his friend on the shoulder.

"You hear that, Skeez? The man says you'll be okay."

Skeezer nodded. "Yeah, great," he whispered in a dry voice.

Kong suddenly appeared at the top of the stage-left ladder and slid down it. He ran to Skeezer's side with a wild-eyed expression. "Is he all right? I just heard."

"I called an ambulance. It ought to be here soon," Joe told him.

"Sit still until it comes," Frank instructed Skeezer. "Sammy, would you stay with him until the ambulance arrives?"

"Sure, man," Sammy said with a nod.

"Let's check out that mike stand, Joe," Frank said.

"I'll kill the power," Kong volunteered, and he ran over to a bank of amplifiers and began flipping switches.

When Kong had finished, Frank used a voltmeter one of the sound men handed him to be sure the mike was dead. Then he picked up the mike stand, and he and Joe began taking it apart.

At that moment Jake appeared from the wings.

Joe, checking over Frank's shoulder, saw that a thin copper wire had been taped to the inside of the mike stand rod, and it was spliced into the main power cable.

"This thing was deliberately wired to electrocute whoever touched the stand," Frank observed.

"And since it was Buddy's mike stand, it's obviously another attempt on Buddy. It was just chance that Skeezer touched it first," Joe said.

Jake had come over and was looking down

at the mike stand in Frank's hands. "I'm glad Skeezer'll be okay," he muttered.

A rising wail in the distance drew Joe's attention away from the mike stand, and he saw an ambulance emerge from access tunnel A and pull up to the stage. White-suited medics got out and put Skeezer onto a stretcher.

As the ambulance drove off Buddy appeared in the doorway of his motor home. "What's going on now?" he shouted. "Don't you realize I need to rest?"

Kong separated himself from the group of roadies around the stage. "You jerk! Skeezer could have died because of you! He grabbed your mike stand and almost got electrocuted!"

"What?" Buddy was stunned. "It was Blade! I know it! That nut won't stop until he gets me! That's it! I'm not performing here! It's too dangerous!"

"Hold on, Buddy," Schacht shouted, running after the rocker, who was rapidly retreating into his motor home. Joe watched as Buddy slipped through the door before Schacht could catch him. Schacht pounded on the door for several moments before Buddy finally let him in.

Joe heard the sounds of a heated argument from inside the motor home, though as before it was impossible to make out who was saying what to whom.

"Well, there goes the ballgame," Joe said

in disgust. "I think Blade may have scared Buddy out of performing in Bayport."

"Yeah, you may be right, Joe," Frank agreed regretfully. "If Buddy just had the guts to hang on, I'm sure Blade would give us another shot at him. I do feel like we're getting closer to catching him even if we don't have any evidence to nail him."

"Hey, look over by tunnel C. Here comes Bobby Mellor waving something," Joe said suddenly.

"He looks pretty excited," Frank observed.

"Where's Syd?" Mellor asked breathlessly.

"He just went into Buddy's motor home, and I have a feeling he'll be there awhile," Joe told him.

"What happened?" Mellor asked with a look of dread on his face.

"Someone rigged Buddy's mike stand and got Skeezer instead," Frank said.

Mellor paled under his deep tan. "Oh, no! Is Skeezer okay?"

"We think so," Frank answered. "He was sitting up when the ambulance came. Didn't you hear the siren?"

"No," Mellor replied. "I've got a temporary office back in the dressing rooms. I can't hear much from in there. But while I was working I heard a thump on my door and thought somebody was knocking. When I opened the door I found this," Mellor said, holding out a note on white paper and another military dagger identical to the first one.

"Was there anyone around when you opened the door?" asked Frank.

Mellor shook his head. "No. By the time I got to the door all I heard was someone a long way off, running. I ran out into the hall and looked, but I couldn't see anybody."

Joe unfolded the slip of white paper. Like the previous notes from Blade, this one was printed in block capital letters in pencil. Joe studied it intently.

> This is a final warning. If Buddy Death performs here, he dies. Nothing and no one will stand in my way.
>
> Blade

"I guess he was pretty sure that mike stand stunt would scare Buddy off if it didn't kill him," Joe commented.

"If Syd manages to get Buddy onstage I'm sure Blade'll try again," Frank commented grimly.

"Hey, can I have that back?" Mellor asked. "I want to show it to Syd."

Joe gave Frank a questioning glance, and Frank nodded, so Joe handed it over. Mellor slipped the note and the dagger into his pocket.

"Maybe you shouldn't let Buddy see that

new note and the dagger," Frank told him. "He's ready to quit now."

"We'll see about that," Mellor told them with a determined gleam in his eye. "Me and Syd have too much riding on this concert to let him quit now."

With that Mellor left, striding quickly toward Buddy's motor home.

After Mellor was out of earshot Joe turned to his brother and said, "I don't like it. Mellor finding that note strikes me as just a little too convenient."

Frank looked skeptical. "You still think Mellor is Blade, huh, Joe?"

"Yes, I do," answered Joe.

"But why, Joe? It's not logical. What would Mellor have to gain? Think of all the money that's been sunk into this tour," Frank insisted.

"But it's Schacht's money that's financing the tour. Mellor doesn't have as much to lose, and maybe he has something to gain," Joe said thoughtfully.

"Like what?" Frank shot back.

"Like maybe Mellor insured Buddy's life for more than he'd make on the tour," Joe suggested.

"Not bad, little brother, and if we can find something like that in Mellor's office, it might be the motive we've been missing."

"Then there's no time like right now for searching his office. He'll probably be in with Buddy and Schacht for a while."

"Okay, you do that," Frank told him, "but make it quick. It could get sticky if Mellor catches you going through his files."

"Don't worry, Frank," Joe replied with a smile. "Let's meet back here in half an hour and compare notes."

"Okay," Frank agreed. "While you're doing that I'll look around to see if I can find any more booby traps."

Joe left the stage and headed for the dressing rooms. He made a right at the corridor junction and went along a curving passage set into the outer wall of the arena that contained the arena offices and dressing rooms. He passed a dozen tan-colored doors until he came to one that had a hand-lettered sign with the name B. Mellor taped to it.

Joe tried the knob to confirm that it was locked. Checking left and right first, he fished his plastic-coated driver's license from his wallet, and after a few tense moments of fiddling with the lock he heard it click open.

He slipped inside and closed the door behind him before flicking on the lights. The first thing he noticed was that Mellor's office was a mess. There were stacks of business papers and newspaper clippings about Buddy Death piled everywhere. Mellor's small desk was stacked with manila file folders and rock magazines. A wide ceramic ashtray in the center of the desk was overflowing with cigarette butts and ashes, and there were half-empty coffee cups sitting on almost every flat surface.

Against one wall was a dart board to which Mellor had pinned a glossy photo of Buddy. There were four darts in the board, all centered around Buddy's head, and the photo had dozens of punctures in it.

"Nice," Joe said to himself, shaking his head.

Joe quickly began going through the manila folders but soon found out that they contained nothing of interest, just contracts with the arena and various companies that had rented equipment to the band. Joe spent ten tense minutes sifting through the pile of folders before giving up on them. He moved on to a cardboard carton in the corner.

He was reaching for the top drawer when he heard footsteps in the corridor. Joe held his breath and noiselessly slid the drawer open.

The first thing he saw was a file marked "Buddy's insurance." He opened the folder and scanned the form for the name of the beneficiary. It was Bobby Mellor.

The footsteps stopped by the door just then, and Joe froze.

Then he heard the jingling of keys being taken from a pocket. Then came the *thunk* of a key being inserted into the lock, and finally the sound of the door handle being slowly turned.

Chapter 8

FRANK ANGRILY POUNDED his fist on the edge of a packing crate. He felt as if he and Joe were getting nowhere and time was running out. He hadn't found any more booby-trapped mike stands, but he knew that sooner or later one of Blade's assassination attempts would succeed.

Frank's mind kept going back to the photos of Blade on the catwalks, their main clue so far. Mentally he turned the images over and over again, wondering if they contained something that he was overlooking.

"No use stewing about it," Frank muttered. He trotted over to the pay phone near the mouth of tunnel A and punched in Callie's number. Remembering that Callie was coming over to the arena that morning to interview Mellor and Schacht, Frank asked her to bring the photos and negatives so he could make better enlargements.

Frank felt slightly better after doing that, but he was so caught up in his thoughts that he almost failed to notice Bobby Mellor leaving Buddy's motor home. By the time Frank was aware of it Mellor was already almost at the entrance of access tunnel C, the one closest to his office.

Oh, no, Frank thought. Joe's still in Mellor's office! He leapt off the stage and raced for Mellor, hoping to stall him long enough for Joe to get out of his office.

Mellor was already so far ahead of him that Frank feared he'd never catch up. He poured on the speed until he skidded to a halt at the junction where tunnel C intersected with the corridor that curved inside the outer wall of the arena. Frank wondered which direction would be quicker, took a guess, and ran to his right.

To his relief, he spotted Mellor a short distance up ahead in the curving passage. Mellor had his hand on the knob of his office door and was just removing his key.

"Mr. Mellor, wait!" Frank shouted.

Startled, Mellor turned to look in the direction of Frank's shout. "What is it, kid? I'm real busy right now."

"Give me a minute to catch my breath," Frank panted, leaning against the wall. His mind raced as he tried to come up with some plausible excuse for stopping Mellor.

"Come on! Come on!" Mellor said impatiently. "What's so important that you nearly busted a gut to catch me, huh?"

Figuring he'd taken his ruse as far as he could, Frank pulled away from the wall where he'd been leaning and told Mellor, "Mr. Schacht sent me to, to, uh, ask you if you had a duplicate set of keys to Buddy's motor home."

Mellor's eyes narrowed suspiciously as he answered, "Sure. But why does Syd want them?"

"Just in case Buddy locks himself in again. Mr. Schacht wants to be able to get right in to talk to him so he doesn't have to waste any time," Frank replied, thinking quickly.

"So he needs my keys to make duplicates, huh?" Mellor said thoughtfully. He detached a set of keys from his ring and held them out to Frank. "Here you go, kid."

Frank made no move to take them but simply shook his head. "Mr. Schacht said he wanted you to bring them to him. I think he said he wanted to talk to you about something."

Mellor threw up his hands in frustration, saying, "When am I going to get my work done?"

Mellor reached for the knob to his office door, and Frank's heart skipped a beat.

It began beating again when he saw Mellor reinsert his key and lock the door before turning in the direction of tunnel C.

"I'd better get back to work, too," Frank said for Mellor's benefit before going a short distance in the opposite direction. He waited until he was sure Mellor had gone, then tiptoed back to the office.

"Joe! It's Frank! Get out of there!" he whispered.

The door popped open, and Frank saw one of Joe's blue eyes shining through the crack. Joe pulled it open wide enough to slip through and carefully locked it behind him.

"That was nice work, Frank," Joe said with a smile. "I thought for sure Mellor was going to catch me when I heard his key in that lock."

"Save the compliments. Let's just get out of here in case Mellor decides to come back. Find anything interesting in there?" Frank asked as he began walking toward tunnel A.

"My hunch about one thing was right," Joe told him. "I found a life insurance policy on Buddy, with Bobby Mellor listed as the beneficiary!"

Frank shrugged. "That doesn't really prove anything. It's probably a normal business precaution. What else did you turn up?"

"I found a photo of Buddy that Mellor was using for a dart board," Joe offered.

"That's no proof, either. We already know Buddy and Mellor don't get along. Did you see anything, anything at all that would link Mellor to Blade?"

"Just those two things and what I already told you about," Joe replied, sounding disappointed.

"Well, we'll need a lot more than that to prove he's Blade," Frank said as they emerged into the bowl of the arena from tunnel A.

"Hey, you Hardys!" someone shouted from the edge of the apron that jutted out from the front of the stage. Frank turned to see Kong hailing them.

"What's up?" Joe called as they walked over to him.

"That pretty blond girl from the Bayport paper came by looking for you guys, but Jake thought it was too dangerous to have her wandering around here. You know, if she was my girlfriend, I'd keep a close eye on her," Kong said with a nasty smile.

"What do you mean by that?" Frank snapped.

Kong shrugged, grinning casually with hostility glittering in his eyes. "I think a girl that pretty needs a real man to take care of her, not some know-it-all schoolboy," he said tauntingly in a low voice.

Frank felt anger surge through him, but he tried to keep it from showing. He knew that Kong was testing him and that the situation could turn violent if he showed any weakness.

"Well, excuse me, Kong," he replied, letting a cold edge of sarcasm creep into his voice. "You must have me confused with someone who cares about your opinion."

With that, Frank turned away, followed by Joe, and started to walk off. Abruptly he stopped and turned to ask Kong, "Where did Jake tell her to wait?"

Kong glared at him for a long moment before sullenly answering, "She's over by the lunch tables."

"Boy, for a second there I thought you and Kong were going to go at it," Joe said as they mounted the stage-right stairs.

"For a second, so did I," Frank admitted.

"What's Callie doing here today, anyway?" Joe asked, changing the subject.

"Since she was coming here to interview Schacht and Mellor, I asked her to bring those photos I took. I thought I'd take another stab at enlarging that design to see if it can tell us anything about Blade."

Joe looked skeptical as they walked across the stage to the lunch table where Callie was waiting.

"Still sounds like a dead end, Frank."

"It's a long shot, but those photos are the

best clue we have to Blade's identity," Frank replied.

"Hi, guys!" Callie said cheerily as soon as she saw them. "Here are your photos, Frank." She handed him the large manila envelope containing the photos and enlargements. Frank opened the envelope and briefly glanced at its contents.

"I'm curious about something," Callie said. "I thought you had decided these pictures were no help."

"I'm going to make another batch of prints on finer-grained paper. I feel that there's something important in them that I'm just missing," Frank said.

"Hey, fellows, we're behind schedule on the new sound tower," Jake interrupted, poking his head around the backdrop at the rear of the stage. "I need all hands right now," he said breathlessly.

"Gee, Jake, I was going to ask if I could have a couple of hours off," Frank responded.

"You've got to be kidding. You'll have to leave, Ms. Shaw. Sorry, but there's going to be a lot of steel flying through the air, and it might get dangerous."

"Okay," Callie replied. "I guess I can interview Mr. Schacht and Bobby Mellor by phone."

"That might be best," Jake agreed. "It's going to get crazy here this afternoon."

She turned to Frank and said, "Call me when you get off tonight, okay?"

"I will," Frank promised. Then, remembering the envelope in his hand, he said, "Since I won't have time to look at these, I want them in a safe place. Would you please put them in the safe in the van?" He reached into his pocket for his keys.

"Okay," Callie agreed, smiling.

Kong suddenly poked his head around the backdrop. "Come on, lover boy. There's hard work to do, and I'm sure you don't want to miss any of it."

Frank glared at Kong, then turned back to Callie. "See you later."

" 'Bye, Callie," Joe shouted over his shoulder. He stopped when he saw Kong run over to Callie. Wordlessly, Joe grabbed Frank's arm and pointed at Kong and Callie.

Frank watched Kong walk up to her wearing an expression that he guessed was Kong's attempt at an ingratiating smile.

"Hi," Kong said. "What you got in the envelope, sweet thing?"

"Photos," Callie snapped, adding in an icy tone, "and I'm not your sweet thing, so watch it, buster, or I'll tell your boss you've been manhandling a reporter."

"Hey, I was just trying to be friendly," Kong said before turning on his heel and stalking off.

A moment later Frank saw Syd Schacht come out of access tunnel B. Callie noticed him, too, and she went right over to him and began talking excitedly. Frank couldn't hear what she was saying, but he guessed from her gestures that she was complaining about Kong.

Suddenly he felt a tug on his shirt and heard Joe whisper, "Come on, Frank. Whether we like it or not we have to work, or we'll blow our cover. Callie can take care of herself."

The two boys walked around to the front of the stage and joined the work gang passing steel to roadies at the base of the tower. They passed along the scaffolding and watched as the gleaming structure was built higher and higher. The boys shared a look. The tower would stay up.

Something was nagging at Frank. Kong was nowhere to be seen, and Frank couldn't help feeling uneasy as he thought of Callie's run-in with the big roadie. Frank abruptly stopped pulling steel from the pile and slapped himself in the forehead.

"What's the matter, Frank?" Joe asked.

"I just remembered. I didn't see the negatives in that envelope. I've got to make sure Callie left them for me, or we're not going to have any new enlargements. Joe, can you cover for me for a few minutes? I'll be right back."

"Sure." Joe shrugged. "After all, it's only rock 'n' roll."

"Thanks," Frank yelled as he ran off to catch Callie.

As soon as he set foot inside the tunnel Frank knew something was wrong. All the lights were out.

"Callie?" Frank yelled. "You in there?"

There was no answer, and a dreadful chill snaked down Frank's spine. He ran down the center of the tunnel as fast as he dared in the pitch darkness, furiously wishing for a flashlight or cat's eyes.

Frank had counted off about fifty paces when he heard the sounds of a struggle off to his right.

"Callie?" he yelled as loud as he could.

He heard a slap, a man's harsh whisper, and then, to his horror, Callie's scream—a scream that was abruptly cut off.

Frank strained to hear in the darkness and ran for the spot where he'd heard the scuffle. Some muffled grunts that sounded like Callie trying to scream with a hand over her mouth came next.

Furious, Frank ran faster, his arms outstretched, hoping to snag Callie's attacker. He heard the man whirl around at the sound of his approach.

"Frank, be careful!" she shouted.

Then suddenly Frank felt a karate chop

strike him at the base of his neck. The blow drove him to his knees, but he managed to grab his assailant's ankles and trip him.

Frank could dimly make out his enemy's dark form as the guy fell with a dull thud. Frank hoped he'd stunned him, but the attacker was up again in an instant and charging Frank with a flurry of karate blows.

Frank spun away and launched a counterattack, aiming kicks and punches where he thought his enemy's head and torso were. The attacker absorbed all the punishment Frank dished out.

They sparred in the darkness for several more tense moments before Frank was driven back by a furious rain of body blows. As he retreated his left heel caught on something and he tumbled backward.

He rolled when he hit and bounced back up again quickly, but his attacker met him with a kick to the head that knocked him flat to the floor.

"Frank! He's got the pictures!" he heard Callie scream before he lost consciousness.

Chapter 9

IT WAS DIFFICULT to hear much of anything over the clank of steel pipes and the orders being shouted, but Joe was sure he'd just heard someone shout, "Help!" He paused and cocked his head to listen, then he knew he'd heard the scream.

Joe threw down the support rod he'd just picked up, startling the other roadies in the crew.

"Hey—what gives, Joe?" asked Tex.

Joe didn't waste his breath answering. He saved it for running flat out across the arena floor toward tunnel A. As he entered the dark tunnel he heard the same female voice scream for help. It was Callie.

"Hang on, Callie! It's Joe. I'm coming!" he shouted.

"Over here, Joe! Hurry! Frank's hurt!" Callie shouted.

Guided by the sound of Callie's voice, Joe quickly found her. He struck a light from a book of matches he had in his pocket and saw Callie kneeling against a wall.

"What happened?" asked Joe.

"The lights went out when I was halfway down the tunnel," she replied. "Then someone attacked me. He got away with the photos and knocked Frank out cold."

The match burned down to Joe's fingers, making him yelp. He lit another one and handed the matches to Callie.

"Light another one so I can find Frank," he instructed.

Callie held the match until Joe found his unconscious brother. He lifted him over his shoulder in a fireman's carry. By the time they reached the tunnel's entrance Frank was starting to come around.

"Did you get the license number of that truck?" Frank muttered.

Joe laughed and knew Frank was all right.

"Frank, are you okay?" Callie asked anxiously.

"He's all right, Callie," Joe answered her, "or he wouldn't be making bad jokes."

Joe set Frank down in a sitting position and leaned him against the inner wall of the arena.

"Frank, did you see who it was?" Joe asked.

Frank rubbed his temples and shook his head.

"Callie, do you know who it was?" Joe asked her.

Callie bit her lip and shook her head.

"I know what you're thinking, Joe," Frank said, "but don't even bother looking for our attacker. I'm sure whoever it was is long gone."

As soon as Frank finished speaking Joe heard a shuffling sound in the dark tunnel.

"I'm not so sure about that, Frank," Joe whispered before he went over to the tunnel entrance. He stood for a few seconds, listening, staring into the darkness. The shuffling grew louder.

Suddenly Jake Williams staggered into view holding one hand to the left side of his head. Jake lurched against a wall, and Joe hurried over to hold him up.

"Jake, what happened?" asked Joe.

"I can't say," Jake mumbled, holding his hand to his left temple and wincing. "I was putting together the compressed-air cannon when the lights went out. While I was looking for the door somebody came up from behind and conked me."

"Someone attacked Frank, too," Joe said

grimly. "Whoever it was, he could still be in the arena."

Jake looked up at Joe for the first time.

"Why don't you wait here until you feel better, Jake?" Joe suggested.

Jake shook his head. "No, I'll be okay. I've been hit worse than this before."

With those words he strode off toward the road crew. As he walked past, Joe noticed an ugly purple bruise starting to form across his temple.

"What really burns me up is that he got the pictures," Frank said after Joe rejoined him. "Now I'll never know what the enlargements might have shown."

"Not necessarily, Frank," Callie quietly told him. "The negatives weren't with the photos. They're still in my purse."

Joe smiled as he watched a broad grin spread across his brother's face. "Callie, you're great!" Frank and Joe said almost together.

Roadies kept stopping by to ask what had happened to Jake. Kong was the last to arrive, sporting a bad bruise on his left cheek.

Joe sauntered over to Kong. "That's a nasty bruise, Kong. What happened?" he asked casually.

Kong glared at him. "Mind your own business, punk," he growled.

"No need to get hostile, Kong," Joe said

easily. "I was just asking. It's not like you to have anything to hide, right?"

Kong whirled on Joe, wearing a wrathful expression. "I—" he began, then swallowed what he was going to say. "Yo, Jake, what happened to you, man?" he asked instead.

"Never mind," Jake replied. "Go see if you can get the lights back on in tunnel A, then check around the main power cables to see what went wrong."

Wordlessly Kong nodded and left.

"Hey, Jake, do you know where Buddy is?" Joe called.

Jake smiled grimly over his shoulder. "Tex told me that when he heard what happened to me he ran back to his motor home and locked himself in. Schacht and one of Hubbard's people are with him."

"What about the other guys in the band?"

"Schacht told them to stay in their dressing rooms. Bobby Mellor's with them, so they ought to be safe."

Callie shuddered. "I just wonder if anybody's safe with this Blade character creeping around attacking people."

"Callie, we don't know for certain it was Blade who attacked us," Frank pointed out.

Casting an uneasy glance at Jake and the other roadies who stood almost within earshot, Joe bent down and suggested, "If we're going to analyze this case, we should go somewhere a little more private."

They got up and moved to the center of the arena floor, at least fifty yards from anyone. Joe said, "Frank, so far this investigation is getting us nowhere. I think we need more background on Buddy."

"Hey, guys, don't forget I'm on this case, too," Callie put in. "Why don't you let me do some of the legwork while you're stuck here?"

"Okay, Callie. See what else you can find on Buddy. Meanwhile I'll make another batch of photos and hope I can get a clearer look at that design. The rap on the head I took is a perfect excuse to take a couple of hours off," Frank said. "I'll just tell Jake I'm going to the doctor."

"What about me?" Joe asked.

"Somebody's got to stay here and maintain our cover, Joe. If all three of us are gone, it might tip Blade off that we're not what we seem to be."

Joe would have preferred developing photos to slinging steel and lugging road cases, but he had to admit that Frank was right. "I'll check around to see if I can dig up anything else," Joe said.

"See you," Frank called, leaving with Callie.

The guys were having a break, so Joe began

to search the perimeter of the arena. As he walked around the outside of the domed space he kept thinking about the bruises he'd seen on Jake and Kong. Frank had said that some of his blows had connected with Blade, and Kong and Jake both had bruises on the left sides of their faces. Frank was right-handed and usually led with his right when they were sparring, Joe remembered. If he hit somebody with a solid right hand, he'd have a bruise on the left side of his face.

Jake had offered a seemingly plausible explanation for his bruise. Kong had offered none at all. Could Kong be Blade?

Joe kicked at an empty paper cup on the ground. He felt angry and helpless. Blade was out there somewhere, he thought, and he and Frank could only guess who he was or where he might strike next.

He and Frank had only suspects, no hard evidence. Buddy's concert was set for the following night. Joe was certain that if they didn't catch Blade before then, he'd strike at Buddy during the show—maybe endangering thousands of innocent fans.

Joe was occupied with those gloomy thoughts when a flash of movement around the corner of a Dumpster caught his eye. He immediately sought cover, then began to ease up to the Dumpster and slide around to its corner. He paused for a moment, gathering himself, then charged around the corner.

"Hold it right there!" Joe shouted to the leather-jacketed back bending over near a door in the outer wall of the arena. The person spun around, wearing a look of utter astonishment. It was David Pauling, the fan who'd been in the arena the night the spotlight had nearly crushed Buddy.

Joe's gaze dropped from Pauling's startled face to his hand. Light glinted off an open switchblade as David came at him.

Chapter 10

"HEY, W-WAIT—" Joe stammered as he took in the gleaming knife blade and David Pauling's wild-eyed expression. There was no time for more than a quick glance. Pauling was only an arm's length away, holding the blade at waist height and close to his side so Joe couldn't knock it away.

As Pauling rushed him Joe pivoted on his left foot and sidestepped the knife. Expecting another attack, he wheeled around to face Pauling again. But to his surprise, Pauling had kept on running toward a gate that led to the parking lot. Joe followed and spotted a beat-up red racing motorcycle through the chain link fence that surrounded the lot, and he guessed it was Pauling's.

"You can't get away that easy," Joe muttered as he took off after Pauling.

Pauling poured on the speed and passed through the gap in the chain link fence into the wide parking lot. Joe caught a glimpse of Pauling's pale face as the teen shot a glance over his shoulder.

Joe ran even faster, trying to close the gap before Pauling got to his motorcycle. The fan zigzagged as he ran, and Joe did gain on him. But just as he stuck out a hand to grab Pauling's shoulder Joe's foot hit an oily patch on the pavement. Both feet slid out from under him, and he slammed into the ground.

"Oooff!" he cried as the air rushed from his lungs.

As he tried to pick himself up he heard a motorcycle engine roar to life. He got to his feet just in time to see Pauling take off across the parking lot and through the lot's wide main gate.

"Nuts!" Joe muttered disgustedly as he watched Pauling disappear down the road. Totally discouraged, Joe limped back to the arena, rubbing the hip he had landed on.

After Frank walked Callie to her car he got into his van and drove to Speedy Photo.

When Frank appeared at the front counter of the photo shop Duke Wampler's long jaw dropped in surprise.

"What are you doing back here?" Duke asked, brushing his long brown hair out of his sleepy-looking eyes.

"I need to make another set of blowups, Duke," Frank said seriously. "It's important that I do it quickly."

"Jeez, Frank, my boss would skin me alive if he knew I was letting you use his enlargers and stuff," Duke said gloomily.

"Okay, okay, I get the message," Frank replied. "Now I owe you a favor. I'll help you study for the final exam in calculus. Fair enough?"

"I guess," Duke replied, a little less gloomy. "All I want is a B in the class so my dad will stay off my back. Help me get a B and we're square."

"No problem," Frank answered.

He and Duke shook on their deal, then Frank asked, "Where do you keep the really fine-grained developing paper, Duke? I've got an idea."

Within a few minutes Frank had put the negative showing Blade's shirt design in the enlarger and was slowly turning the focus knob, trying for the clearest image possible.

He raised the head of the enlarger by turning a hand crank on its side, then turned the focus knob a fraction of an inch before he was satisfied.

Acting on a sudden inspiration, Frank overexposed the image slightly, hoping to bring out some of the detail in the design that had been lost in shadow. Then he made six more prints of the enlargement, varying the exposure times so that he would have the greatest possible range of dark to light values in the photos.

He finished his enlargements and slipped the first photo into the shallow tray of developing bath.

As the first image emerged from the blank paper Frank felt a thrill of satisfaction. He'd been right about a finer-grained paper bringing out greater detail. Without waiting for the photo to dry he took it into the next room, where he could examine it under bright light with a magnifying glass.

The details of the design were clearly visible. Frank saw an intricate flowing piece of artwork that seemed oddly familiar, though he wasn't quite sure if it was a T-shirt or something else entirely.

Frank went back into the darkroom and pulled the other prints out of the developer tank. He had five new 8 x 10 prints showing large, clear images of the design.

He was at the front counter scrutinizing them under Duke's magnifying glass when the phone rang. Duke took the call, then handed the phone to Frank. "Here. It's for you."

"Hi, it's Joe." His voice sounded faint on

the other end of the line. "They need you at the arena."

"What's up?"

"Buddy was too jumpy to play, so Schacht canceled this afternoon's rehearsal. He wants us to drive the band back to their hotel so they can rest up before the press conference tonight."

"I'll be right there," Frank assured him. "I think I've finally found a decent clue in my photo."

"Great!" Joe replied. "See you soon."

After thanking Duke for the use of the lab Frank gathered up his photos and raced back to the arena.

When Frank parked the van he saw Buddy's motor home and a black stretch limousine parked near an exit. Joe lounged against the side of the motor home while Schacht and Bobby Mellor stood tensely beside the limousine, checking their watches and talking into Mellor's walkie-talkie. Frank locked the van and trotted over to join them.

"About time you got here!" Mellor snapped at him.

"I came from the doctor's office as soon as I got Joe's message," Frank replied.

"How's your head, Frank?" asked Schacht.

"We can talk about it later, Mr. Schacht," Frank replied.

"Yeah, later is a good time to talk about it," Mellor said impatiently as Joe joined the group. "I'd like to get our star to his hotel before he has a nervous breakdown."

"I'm ready whenever you are," Frank said to Mellor, a note of irritation creeping into his voice. "What do you want us to do, Mr. Schacht?"

"I want you to drive the limo, Frank," Schacht told him. "I fired the driver. Buddy's inside with Sammy and Eric. I'll ride with them. Joe will follow in Buddy's motor home with Bobby. I figured having you two drive the vehicles would be safest. I know neither of you is Blade."

"Syd, can we get this circus rolling, please?" asked Mellor.

"Take it easy, Bobby," Schacht said firmly. "Getting bent out of shape won't help anybody."

"Which hotel, Mr. Schacht?" Joe asked.

"They're staying at the Branford Towers," Mellor cut in.

"We'll get everybody there safely. Don't worry," Frank said. He opened the door of the limousine. As Schacht climbed inside Frank saw that Joe was already behind the wheel of the motor home, with Mellor sitting next to him in the passenger seat. Joe gave him a thumbs-up sign to show that he was ready to go. Frank slid behind the wheel of the limo.

The car's engine started up with a powerful roar, and Frank threw it into gear. It took him a few moments to get used to the handling of the long car, but it was easy once he caught on.

Frank had never driven a stretch limousine before and marveled at all the features on the dashboard, from the phone to rows of switches that controlled the windows, sun roof, and door locks. Frank experimentally flicked a switch, and the glass panel separating him from the passenger cabin slid down noiselessly.

"Hey, how's it going, dude?" came Sammy's cheerful voice from the backseat.

"Hey, what's going on?" Schacht asked.

"I was just checking out the dashboard," Frank replied a little sheepishly.

"Well, concentrate on your driving and give us some privacy," Buddy said in a haughty voice.

"Yes, sir!" Frank retorted, flicking the switch for the panel. What a creep, Frank thought. That jerk never lets up.

Frank drove on in silence, concentrating on the extra-long vehicle. He got on the highway encircling Bayport and headed toward the exit for the center of town. He turned off at the downtown exit ramp and hit the brake.

As he turned onto the off ramp the brake pedal sank all the way to the floor with no slackening of the limo's speed. "Uh-oh!" Frank said out loud. He stomped on the brake pedal again. No effect.

"Slow down, Frank!" Schacht's voice crackled over the intercom.

"Uh, that might be a problem, Mr. Schacht! The brakes don't work!"

"What!" came a chorus of panicky voices over the intercom.

Frank felt a flash of fear, then remembered the emergency brake. He pulled it back, but the handle came off in his hand. Frank looked at it in horror for a split second before tossing it aside.

"Do something, you moron!" Buddy shouted over the intercom.

Frank kept a tight grip on the wheel. The big car sped down the off ramp, heading straight into oncoming traffic!

Chapter 11

"WHOA!" Frank didn't hear himself shout as the limousine careened out of control, speeding straight at a delivery truck. His heart in his throat, Frank spun the wheel hard to the right. The tires screeched as the big car veered back into its own lane, hit the guard rail, and bounced away.

Grimacing with the effort, Frank leaned on the wheel, forcing the fender against the guard rail in a screaming shower of sparks and tortured metal. Seventy-five yards down the road the car finally slowed to a jerky stop.

Watching from the driver's seat of the motor home, Joe felt relief flood through him.

"Way to go, Frank! Way to go!" Joe exulted.

"I saw it, but I don't believe it!" Mellor said with wonder.

Joe guided the big black-and-white motor home around the other car and parked it on the shoulder of the road. Before Joe had completely stopped Mellor was on the car phone calling for taxis to pick up the band.

As Joe climbed down from the motor home he saw Frank emerge from the limousine and disappear under the front of the car. Joe hurried to join his brother.

"Frank, are you okay?"

"Just scared out of three years' growth," came the muffled reply from under the hood.

Joe knelt down by Frank's legs so he could talk to him more easily over the roar of the passing traffic. Some passenger cars with teenagers in them, attracted by the sight of Buddy's motor home, slowed to a crawl, and the kids shouted and honked their horns.

"Heeey, Buddy! We love you, dude! Buddy rules!" the teenagers shouted.

Joe glanced over at them and shook his head.

"Do you think those kids would love Buddy if they knew the guy?" he wondered aloud.

Frank didn't reply. All Joe heard was a thoughtful "hmmm" coming from his brother. It was followed by a triumphant, "Aha! I knew it!"

A moment later Frank crawled out from

under the car with a smudge of grease on his cheek, rubbing his hands together to clean them off.

"What did you find?" Joe inquired.

"Someone fixed the brakes for us," Frank replied, wiping the grease from his face with a handkerchief. "They punched a tiny hole in the brake line so that I'd have normal brakes for a mile or two. Then as I lost brake fluid in traffic—*whammo*, major accident. I wonder who had access to this car."

"I got there only a few minutes before you did," Joe answered. "We'll have to ask Schacht."

The Hardys went over to the side window of the limo and knocked. The tinted window lowered several inches. They could see Syd Schacht's face through the gap. It was drawn and pale.

"What's up now, boys?" Schacht asked.

"Can we talk to you privately?" Joe asked.

Schacht nodded and climbed out. He came around to the front of the limo and knelt down by the front wheels. Joe and Frank knelt down and joined him.

"Mr. Schacht, was this limo left unattended at any time before we left?" Frank asked.

Schacht considered his question for a moment. "No. Either Bobby or I was beside it or in it at all times until the band arrived."

"Let's check with Mellor," Joe suggested, heading for the motor home.

When Joe pulled open the driver's-side door Mellor, who was talking on the car phone, looked over, annoyed.

"What is it?" he snapped.

"Mr. Mellor, did you leave the limo alone before the band arrived?" Joe inquired.

Mellor held the phone to his chest while he answered. "Well, yeah. A few minutes after Syd left Kong came out and told me I had a call on one of the pay phones in tunnel A."

"Who called you?" Frank asked.

"I don't know. By the time I got there the line was dead," Mellor answered.

"Thanks for the info, Mr. Mellor," Joe told him before closing the door.

"That few minutes when the limo was unattended had to be when the brakes were tampered with," Frank speculated.

"Unless Mellor was lying about the phone call and he monkeyed with the brakes himself," Joe countered.

"Then again, it could have been Kong," Frank guessed.

Joe shrugged. "Maybe, but maybe somebody else put him up to getting Mellor away."

Joe's speculations were cut off by the arrival of a pair of sedans bearing the Bayport

Taxi Company logo, followed by a lumbering tow truck.

While Frank oversaw the limo getting hooked onto the back of the tow truck Joe checked the motor home's brakes to make sure that they hadn't been tampered with.

Buddy and the other band members piled into one taxi. "I'll ride in the motor home with Joe," Frank volunteered as Bobby Mellor climbed into the second taxi with Schacht.

The drive to the Branford Towers was uneventful, for which Joe was thankful. But when he pulled up in front of the hotel Joe noticed a large crowd of Buddy Death fans wearing BDB T-shirts and holding up a large homemade banner that read: Buddy—We Love You!

Joe drove to the underground parking lot, and the crowd of teenagers surged around the vehicle.

He gazed out over the sea of bodies wearing T-shirts that bore Buddy's face or the band's logo, then looked over and noticed Frank's concerned expression.

"Maybe we should have parked this thing on the next block, Joe," Frank said quietly.

"They'll leave us alone when they realize neither of us is Buddy," Joe said.

"Let's hope so," Frank muttered.

Joe grinned. "Relax. The worst thing that'll

happen is a bunch of girls will tear your shirt off. How bad can that be?"

The fans had surrounded the motor home while Joe parked it and were pounding on the sides, chanting, "We want Buddy!" Frank and Joe were mobbed as soon as they opened the doors.

"Hold on a minute! Buddy's not here! We're just on the crew!" Frank shouted to the fans who pressed in, tugging on his clothes.

After a few minutes the Hardys finally made it into the elevator. When they arrived at the top floor of the hotel, where Schacht had reserved an eight-room suite for Buddy and the band, Frank and Joe found a pair of huge, muscular men wearing dark warm-up suits flanking the door to the suite. One had short blond hair. The other had dark hair and a neatly trimmed beard. Both wore no-nonsense expressions.

"Hi," Joe said. "We're Frank and Joe Hardy. We're here to see Mr. Schacht."

The dark-haired man checked a small notebook, then nodded to his companion, saying, "It's okay, Matt. They're on the list."

The other man grunted and opened the door for the Hardys, slamming it as soon as they were inside.

"Wow. Not bad." Joe whistled as the brothers surveyed the wide, expensively carpeted corridor with closed doors leading off at regular intervals.

"Plenty of privacy," Frank remarked. "This suite must take up at least a quarter of the floor." Down the corridor to their right the brothers heard loud talking and the clink of ice in glasses. They followed the sound to a large sunken living room at the end of the corridor. It was filled with comfortable-looking leather couches, glass-and-chrome coffee tables, and a black baby grand piano. Schacht was sprawled on one couch drinking a cup of coffee, and Bobby Mellor was hunched up on the edge of another couch, staring tensely at the phone on the table in front of him.

"Hi, Mr. Schacht," Joe announced from the top of the steps leading down into the living room.

Schacht looked up in surprise. "What kept you boys?"

"We ran into a mob of Buddy's fans in the garage and had to wade through them," Frank replied. "Say, who are the two gorillas outside?"

"Buddy's bodyguards."

Suddenly Joe heard the sound of a door opening. He flicked a quick look down the corridor to his right and saw Buddy come out of his room, followed by Sammy and Eric.

"Yo, dudes! What's happening?" Sammy

called cheerily. Behind Sammy, Eric wore a worried expression.

Buddy sauntered past the Hardys without a word and stepped down into the living room. He went right to the phone.

"Did you tell room service that I don't eat meat?" Buddy asked.

"Buddy, sweetheart, don't worry. Uncle Syd takes care of everything," Schacht told him in a soothing voice.

Buddy tossed his tangled black mop of hair, put the phone to his ear, and began ordering.

"And I want fresh hummus. And send up some bottles of mineral water," he said, finishing his order.

"I'll be in my room resting up for the press conference," Buddy told them. "All this excitement has got my nerves ragged. I want to look good tonight."

As Buddy was leaving Sammy went down into the room to ask Schacht, "Hey, Mr. Money—any word on Skeezer?"

Schacht's answer was interrupted by the phone ringing. Mellor snatched it up before the first ring ended.

"Hello?" he spat out.

Then suddenly Joe saw the tense expression leave Mellor's face. He smiled broadly.

"That was Skeezer. They're letting him out of the hospital. He'll be okay for tomorrow night's show."

"All right!" Sammy shouted.

With a flourish he produced a pair of drumsticks from the back pocket of his frayed jeans and beat a rapid drum roll down the corridor walls to Buddy's door.

"Hey, Buddy!" he shouted. "Skeezer's okay!"

"Great, Sammy," Buddy said impatiently. "Leave me alone."

Sammy made a face at the door, then looked back down the corridor with a grin.

"I'm feeling restless. Hey, you Hardys! Eric! Let's party! My buddy Skeezer's coming home!"

Joe followed Eric into Sammy's room, with Frank trailing him. Although the band had been in Bayport for only two days, Joe saw that Sammy had already turned his room into a shambles. A lamp was overturned, and there were clothes, drums, and empty food containers strewn everywhere. Sammy swept a pile of clothes off the bed and offered it to his guests with a low bow.

"Uh-oh," Eric said with a slow grin. "Sammy's on a roll. Bear with him, guys. He always gets like this before a show."

For the next ten minutes Sammy entertained all three of them with a stream of jokes, funny stories, and snatches of songs. Joe relaxed and began enjoying himself for the first time in two days. If this was stage fright, it wasn't so bad, he told himself. Sammy should perform more often.

"So then Bowie said to me—" Sammy stopped in midsentence when he heard a knock at the front door of the suite. Joe saw a devilish gleam appear in his eyes. Then he leapt up and ran out of the room.

"What's up?" asked Joe with a grin.

"With Sammy, your guess is as good as mine," Eric replied.

Sammy reappeared a moment later carrying a covered tray of food.

"Here's Buddy's food. Let's play a joke on him," Sammy said, chortling.

"I don't think that's a good idea, Sammy," Frank told him. "Buddy's edgy enough right now."

"No, no, it's cool," Sammy insisted. "Buddy could use a good joke. It'll loosen him up for the press conference."

"What are you going to do?" Joe asked.

"Nothing too rotten," Sammy chuckled. "I'll just eat his lunch myself and send Mr. Health Food a treat from my room."

Sammy scanned the room until he spotted a tray shoved under the nightstand, where the maid must have missed it.

"Perfect!" Sammy dived for the tray. He came up with a day-old cheeseburger and a pile of limp, greasy fries.

"Come on, Sammy," Frank insisted. "I really don't think Buddy will laugh at this."

"Sure he will," Sammy replied. "It's in excellent taste!"

Sammy wolfed down Buddy's hummus, pita bread, tabbouleh, and steamed vegetables, but no one laughed.

"No kidding, he'll love this," the rocker insisted as he started out the door with the room service tray containing the stale burger and fries. He never made it to the door. Joe heard a choking sound, and the next thing he knew, Sammy had dropped the tray.

"What happened?" Joe got up to help. Sammy clutched his throat, making gagging noises. His freckled face turned pale. He was having trouble breathing. He coughed again and fell forward into Joe's arms.

"Frank," Joe cried. "Buddy's food was poisoned!"

Chapter 12

Frank was at Joe's side almost before he caught the choking musician.

"Set him down easy, Joe. I'll call an ambulance," Frank instructed.

Frank dashed over to the phone. He told the dispatcher that there had been a poisoning and requested an ambulance.

"What happened?" Eric was bending over Sammy, terrified.

"Buddy's lunch must have been poisoned," Joe guessed. "Go tell Schacht and Mellor. Let them know an ambulance is on the way."

"Check," Eric simply said, and then vanished through the door.

Frank knew that Sammy shouldn't be moved until proper medical care arrived, so he only rolled the unconscious rocker onto his side to keep a close watch on his breathing.

Schacht and Mellor appeared in the doorway. Schacht mopped his bald head with his handkerchief while Mellor stared at Sammy with a horrified expression and wrung his hands.

"Eric told us," Schacht said. "How is he, Frank?"

"He's alive. That's all I know," Frank said without looking up.

The paramedics arrived soon after, and they put Sammy on a gurney and wheeled him down the hall.

As they passed Buddy's door he stuck his head out and peevishly asked, "What's all the racket? I'm trying to re—"

Buddy's words faltered when he saw Sammy being wheeled past.

"W-what happened to Sammy?" he asked in a soft voice.

"He got poisoned eating your lunch," Eric told him crossly.

Buddy turned a shade paler than usual before he slammed his door and locked it.

"Syd!" he screamed through the door. "Get in here."

As the medics pushed Sammy through the door Frank realized that if Blade was indeed responsible for the poisoning, he might have left some clues in the hotel kitchen. "Joe!" he called. "Let's check the kitchen."

Frank and Joe rode to the ground floor with Sammy and the medics. As the elevator doors slid open the Hardys took off through the lobby toward the kitchen. They burst through a pair of swinging doors, startling a chef, who dropped a mixing bowl full of dough.

"What are you kids doing in here?" he demanded angrily.

"One of your guests was just poisoned. Where is the room service food prepared?" Frank asked sharply.

The chef's mouth dropped open, and he simply pointed to a cook's prep station in the corner of the kitchen, where a male and female chef were bustling around half a dozen room service carts.

"But I don't think *they'd* do it. They've been with the hotel for years and their credentials are perfect," the chef said.

Frank started to stride over to the station, but Joe grabbed his arm to stop him.

"Look over at the dishwashing station, Frank," Joe told him, pointing to a bored-looking teenager loading a big industrial dishwasher with racks of dirty plates.

"I don't see—" Frank began, then he stopped as soon as he recognized the dishwasher. "It's David Pauling!" he whispered.

"Maybe he poisoned Buddy's food," Joe suggested.

"There's only one sure way to find out," Frank replied.

Frank and Joe quietly slipped up behind Pauling, who was concentrating on his work.

"David Pauling—we want to talk to you," Joe told him firmly.

Pauling spun around, wide-eyed, and tried to bolt past them. Joe caught him easily and pushed him back against the dishwashing machine.

"You're not going anywhere until you answer a few questions, David," Joe told him.

"I didn't do anything! Honest!" Pauling said in panic.

"Take it easy," Frank assured him, coming a step closer. "We just want to talk to you."

"What's going on here, eh?" a voice asked behind them.

Frank looked for the speaker and saw the first chef glaring at him.

"Somebody from the Buddy Death Band got poisoned a few minutes ago," Frank explained. "We've seen David at the arena twice, both times after accidents. We think he might have something to do with the poisoning."

The chef snorted contemptuously. "That's ridiculous. David is no murderer!"

"How long have you been here today?" Joe demanded.

"He came on at two," the chef told them before Pauling had a chance to answer. "Here, I'll show you," he said, leading the Hardys over to a time clock and a rack of cards.

He pulled out the one bearing the name David Pauling and shoved it under Frank's nose. Frank saw that David had clocked in at 2:03 P.M.

Frank then asked the chef, "Is there some record of when the room service orders go out?"

The chef's head bobbed up and down. With a curt wave he led the Hardys over to a wire spindle at the room service station and pawed through the stack of orders before extracting one and handing it to Frank. Frank checked it out and saw that the order had come in at 1:22 and had gone out at 1:47, almost fifteen minutes before David Pauling had clocked in.

"Are you sure David clocked in at two?" Frank asked the chef.

"Positive," the man replied. "I remember, because I scolded him for being three minutes late."

"Did anyone else see him come in then?" Joe asked.

The chef turned to the male and female prep cooks, who'd stopped working and were staring at them with interest. "What about it, Carol? Ralph?"

"It was just after two. I remember because you were standing under the big clock over the kitchen entrance while you chewed David out."

The chef glanced back at the Hardys with a satisfied expression. "There. Three witnesses. Is that enough?"

"I guess this puts David in the clear about the poisoning," Joe agreed. "But I still want to know why he lied to Captain Hubbard about being unemployed."

"Well?" Frank asked.

Pauling fidgeted and stared down at his feet before answering. "I didn't want to tell anybody where I worked 'cause I just got this job, and I was afraid that if I got in trouble I'd get fired."

"Why did you try to knife me at the arena earlier?" Joe asked, fixing David with a hard stare.

"I—I—" David stammered. "I didn't want to hurt you, man. You just surprised me, and I wanted to get away."

"You were warned not to come back to the arena. What were you doing there?" Frank asked.

"I thought maybe if I sneaked inside I could talk to Buddy and let him know that I'd never hurt him. That's all. I just wanted to talk to my man Buddy. Honest!" he added, his eyes wide.

"Why did you have a knife in your hand?" Joe persisted.

"To jimmy the door lock so I could sneak in without the arena cops grabbing me."

Frank realized that questioning Pauling was fruitless. He turned back to the trio of cooks.

"Did anybody else notice anything out of the ordinary around the time Buddy's order went out?" Frank asked, scanning their faces.

The female cook, a petite, dark-haired woman, spoke first. "I remember thinking we had a new waiter—one I didn't recognize. Come to think of it, he was the one who took the order up to Buddy Death's suite."

"What did he look like?" Joe jumped in excitedly.

She shrugged. "I only noticed him out of the corner of my eye. All I remember was that he was a big guy in a waiter's jacket."

"Where's the service elevator?" Frank asked.

"Through there." The chef pointed toward some battered steel swinging doors in the far corner of the room.

"Let's check it out," Frank suggested.

The brothers went through the doors. Facing them was the gray service elevator. To their right was a pair of swinging doors like the ones they'd just opened.

Frank turned and called over his shoulder, "Where do those other doors lead?"

"To a service corridor that leads to the rear of the lobby," the chef answered.

Joe opened the doors and peered into the corridor.

"Frank, I found something!" he shouted.

Frank followed him into the corridor. He found Joe bending over an industrial ice machine set in a niche in the wall.

As Frank watched, Joe pulled something out of the narrow space between the side of the ice machine and the wall.

"Look at this." Joe held up a wrinkled red waiter's jacket and black pants. "Blade could have changed out of this waiter's outfit on his way to the lobby after delivering the poisoned food."

"If you're right," Frank pointed out, "then Buddy's bodyguards should be able to give us a decent description of the guy."

As they pushed through some swinging doors into the lobby Joe said, "I don't care if there was a poisoning, I'm starved. Before we quiz the bodyguards, how about getting a couple of burgers?"

"As long as they're not from room service," Frank agreed.

As the Hardys crossed the Branford's wide lobby to the coffee shop Joe suddenly grabbed Frank's arm and pointed to the front entrance.

Syd Schacht was standing just inside the door, scanning the lobby. He quickly spotted the Hardys and crossed to join them.

"Blade is back," Schacht said grimly. "A couple of minutes after you left we found a note outside the suite."

"Another threat against Buddy?" Frank asked.

"No. This time he threatened to get you and your brother if you don't lay off. I'll show it to you when you come up."

"We'll be right there," Frank informed him. "Your bodyguards may be able to give a description of Blade. They probably took the tray of food from him."

When Schacht had gone the brothers eyed each other. "Let's hit the coffee shop," Frank said.

As they stepped inside the restaurant Frank spotted a familiar couple in the farthest booth.

"Say, Joe, isn't that—" Frank began.

"Jake and Clare Williams?" Joe said, completing Frank's sentence. "It sure is."

"Let's see if we can get close enough to hear what they're talking about," Frank said quietly.

"Lead on," Joe responded.

Jake's attention was totally occupied with his sister. It was easy for Frank and Joe to sneak across the crowded coffee shop and slip into a booth behind them.

"So what are you going to do about those poems, Clare? They're yours!" Jake was saying.

"Just drop it, Jake, okay?" she said wearily. "I'm tired of fighting about it."

"Well, if you're not here about the poems, you're here to see him, aren't you?"

"I—" Clare began defensively.

"I knew it!" Jake said tightly. "Stay away from Buddy, Clare. That's an order. I won't have you chasing after him, living in rat traps like that Star-Lite Motel. Once the tour starts it could be dangerous just to be around that creep. Sammy just got poisoned, and who knows who'll be next?"

"But I—" the pretty girl began.

Jake's voice rose hysterically. "You hear me, Clare? You stay away!"

Chapter 13

"YOU'RE MY BROTHER, not my boss!" Clare flared angrily. "I'll go where I please and see who I want!"

"I'm telling you for your own good!" Jake shouted louder.

Joe noticed Jake's tool bag on the floor beside him. Sticking out of the unzipped top was a bright orange lineman's phone, the type telephone repairpeople carry to tap into phone lines. Joe wondered why Jake would be carrying that around, but his train of thought was interrupted when Clare suddenly sprang from her seat. "I don't have to take this, Jake! I'm going back to my motel!"

"Good!" Jake shouted, following her out. "You stay there until Buddy leaves town!"

When he was sure Jake had gone Joe spoke to Frank. "What do you make of that?" he asked.

"What Jake said about it being dangerous to be around Buddy?" Frank replied.

"It sounded like he knows more than he's saying."

"Yeah," Frank agreed. "Something else bothered me, too. How did Jake know about Sammy so fast?"

"We'd better check whether someone told him," Joe said. He looked at his watch. "Let's get our food and head upstairs."

When Frank and Joe got back to the band's suite they found a pair of Bayport police officers quizzing Schacht and the two bodyguards. To Joe's relief, one of the officers was Con Riley, a friend of the Hardys. Joe knew Con to be fair and hoped he would give them the elbow room they'd need to help solve the case.

"I don't really see how I can keep a lid on this, Mr. Schacht," he overheard Con saying. "Attempted murder is serious business."

"All I'm asking for is a little cooperation to keep these incidents quiet until after Buddy's concert," Schacht pleaded.

Con Riley didn't appear to be persuaded. "Well . . ." he hedged.

Joe saw an opportunity to jump into the conversation, and he took it. "Con, Frank and I are working on tracking Blade down."

"In fact, these two bodyguards may have seen Blade," Frank quickly added. "Did they give you a description of the room service waiter?"

"I can answer that, kid," the blond bodyguard replied in a gravelly voice. "The waiter was a big guy, over six feet tall, with dark hair and a bushy beard."

"Could be almost anyone with a wig and fake beard," Con noted.

I can think of at least two people it could be, Joe thought to himself. He could tell from Frank's expression that the same thought had occurred to his brother.

"I agree it's not enough of a description to pin the poisoning on anybody, but we've narrowed our list down to only a few suspects. All we need is a little more time to unmask Blade."

"And would you mind telling me who the suspects are?" Con asked sarcastically.

Frank appeared to be uncomfortable. "Right now our evidence is too thin for us to make any accusations. That's why I asked for more time before we name names."

"Well, you boys have a pretty good track record. Mr. Schacht has confidence in you. I'll tell you what. I won't interfere with you yet on this case. But I'm assigning extra officers to the arena. At the first sign of danger to the public I'll stop the show. In the meantime, we'll keep a lid on everything."

"Great! That's great, Officer Riley. Thanks a lot," Syd Schacht said. Then he turned to the bodyguards. "Everything said here is confidential, fellows. Nobody's to know the Hardys are working for me."

Wordlessly the big men nodded.

"Thanks, Con. You won't be sorry," Joe said.

Con gave Joe and Frank a skeptical look as he and the other officer left the room. I hope not, he seemed to be thinking.

As soon as the two police officers had left Schacht turned to the Hardys. "Okay, you wouldn't tell the cops who your suspects are, but I have to know—is it someone on my staff?"

"There are several possibilities," Joe answered, "but it's probably better that we don't tell you who they are right now."

"Why not? I'm trustworthy!"

"That's not what's in doubt, Mr. Schacht," Frank cut in. "If we tell you who our prime suspects are, you might accidentally tip the real Blade off. We want to sneak up on him so nobody else gets hurt."

"Well, as long as you can keep things quiet, I'll let you run this investigation your own way," Schacht told them.

"You can help a lot by making sure Buddy's bodyguards stick to him like glue, just in case Blade gets past us," Joe said seriously.

"Don't worry, I'll keep Buddy under wraps," Schacht said. "Now, you guys better get back to the arena. I want to make sure there are no surprises at tonight's press conference."

To Joe's annoyance, he and Frank had to share a taxi with Bobby Mellor on the ride back to the arena, making it impossible for the Hardys to discuss the case.

Joe's frustration doubled when he and Frank were separated as soon as they arrived at the arena. Jake sent Frank to work with the sound crew in the tech booth suspended over the center of the arena.

Joe was assigned to the crew in charge of the smoke machines. He waited in the wings for the climax of the special effects display, at which time he was supposed to drop a twenty-pound block of dry ice into the smoke machine's tank of water. Carbon dioxide fog would be pumped through a tube to create a thick white wall of "smoke."

Joe spotted Callie sitting onstage in a metal folding chair with about twenty other print and television reporters. She would be covering the press conference for the paper.

Syd Schacht had arranged for the media people to sit in the center of the stage so they could get a clear view of the spectacular light show that would accompany Buddy's performance the following night.

To Joe's relief, the press conference went smoothly. Joe had to admit that Buddy, Skeezer, and Eric handled themselves well. Buddy in particular took to the limelight like a pro. He appeared charming, funny, and humble as he answered questions and posed for pictures.

If I didn't know better, I wouldn't believe it was the same guy who's been behaving like a jerk for the last two days, Joe thought.

The press conference climaxed with the special effects preview, the moment that had Joe worried as the most likely for Blade to strike.

From beside his smoke machine Joe kept a close eye on Buddy. He knew Frank was high up in the tech booth, scanning the catwalks with binoculars. The brothers kept in contact with walkie-talkies that Schacht had given them. Con Riley had sent a dozen officers to guard the arena.

Joe hoped that the increased security might scare Blade off, but then he recalled Blade's notes. Blade was determined to stop Buddy—no matter what the cost.

After the final laser display Schacht and Bobby Mellor ushered the press out of the arena. Callie waved to Frank and Joe as they joined the other roadies in cleaning up the stage and making sure all the lights and other equipment were ready for the concert.

It was well after two A.M. when Jake finally told Joe he could go home. He'd have to report for work at six P.M. the next day, though. Joe was so tired he could scarcely keep his eyes open. When he spotted his brother slowly coming down the stage-left ladder, Joe knew Frank was just as tired.

Joe saw the arena lights go out as he and Frank wearily trudged down tunnel A to the parking lot and through the knots of teenagers waiting for the show the next night.

"Boy, I thought I couldn't wait to talk about the case with you, Frank, but now all I want to do is fall into bed."

"I can't even think straight," Frank agreed. "Maybe we should wait and discuss it with Callie over breakfast."

Joe was still dressing when Callie arrived at the Hardy home the next day at two o'clock. He pulled on a clean T-shirt and greeted her from the top of the stairs. "Morning, Callie. Thanks for joining us for breakfast."

"Good *afternoon,* Joe. I'm not just joining you, I'm the chef, Mr. Hardy," Callie replied smartly. "I figured I'd better give you two at least one decent meal while your mom and aunt are out of town. I'm making western omelets, whole wheat toast, and juice. How's that sound?"

"Great, especially since I don't have to cook it," Joe replied with a smile.

"Oh, did you hear? Sammy's going to be okay. They got his stomach pumped soon enough."

Joe smiled again. That was a relief.

While Callie dished up the steaming omelets filled with chunks of ham, green pepper, and onion, Frank and Joe filled her in on everything they'd learned so far.

"Have you eliminated David Pauling and Bobby Mellor as suspects?" Callie inquired.

"Well, Mellor does hate Buddy, but he's got a lot riding on the success of this concert, so it doesn't make sense that Mellor would threaten his own interests. Besides, Mellor was with Schacht when Buddy's food arrived. Unless he was working with an accomplice, he couldn't have poisoned Buddy's food," Frank pointed out.

Callie thought for a minute. "Well, you said David Pauling worked in the hotel kitchen. Could he be Blade's accomplice?"

"Pauling came on his shift after the bogus waiter picked up Buddy's food, so that eliminates him," Joe said, shoveling in the last bites of his omelet.

"Then what about the two times Pauling

showed up at the arena, Joe? He did attack you with a knife!" Callie's voice rose excitedly.

Joe smiled slightly. "It was a pretty lame knife attack, Callie. He was just trying to get away. My guess is that Pauling is just a victim of lousy timing. He's always in the wrong place at the wrong time."

"Then if neither of them is Blade, Jake and Kong are the only reasonable suspects, right?" Callie ventured.

"That makes sense, Callie. Those two are the only ones who would match the size of the fake waiter," Joe put in quickly.

"The tactics and booby traps Blade has used so far indicate some kind of military training, which both Jake and Kong have had," Frank observed.

"Yeah, but didn't you learn that Kong was a SEAL?" Callie asked. "I'd say that meant he knew more about booby traps and ambushes than Jake."

Frank considered that while sipping his orange juice, then finally said, "True, but Jake specialized in demolition. That tells me he probably knows something about booby traps, too."

"All I know is that Kong gives me the creeps," Callie said with a small shudder. "My gut feeling is that he's probably Blade."

"Well, so far everything we have is just circumstantial. We can't go around making accusations against that tattooed ape without solid proof,'' Joe reminded her.

Suddenly Joe snapped his fingers. ''Tattoos! Hey, Frank—where did you leave those photos of Blade?''

''They're in my room. Why? Did you get an inspiration?''

Joe shrugged. ''More of a hunch, really. But I think I can prove who Blade is.''

Joe ran to Frank's room, where he grabbed the photo blowups and a magnifying glass. Joe then hurried downstairs to his father's office, tossed the envelope onto the desk, and began scanning the bookshelves for the specific title he needed.

He spied it on a bottom shelf and pulled out the thick volume covered in a glossy dust jacket. After he found the page he was looking for he pulled the photos from the envelope.

With growing excitement Joe compared the glossy color photo in the book to the design in Frank's photo.

''That's it!'' he said triumphantly.

He snatched up the photo and ran back to the kitchen. ''Frank, Callie, I've got it!''

''What've you got, Joe?'' Frank asked.

Waving the photo at them, Joe said excitedly, ''The proof that Kong is Blade!''

Chapter 14

FRANK FELT A THRILL of excitement, but his natural caution asserted itself immediately.

"Let's see the proof," Frank said calmly.

"It's here in this picture you took, Frank," Joe replied excitedly. "It was here all along. We were just interpreting it wrong."

Frank examined the enlarged design in the photo again but saw nothing new. "Okay, Joe," Frank said carefully. "What about this T-shirt design makes you think it's Kong in the photo?"

"That's the whole thing, Frank—it's not a T-shirt design! It's a tattoo!"

Frank's jaw dropped in disbelief. "Of course! Kong is covered with tattoos! If he's got one that matches this one, that's our proof!"

"Great work, Joe!" Callie told him excitedly. "What made you think of tattoos?"

"Well," Joe answered, "something about that design struck me as familiar. I remembered a book on tattooing that our dad used to break a case a few years back, and something clicked. I compared the tattoo in the photo to one of the Japanese Yakuza-style tattoos, and they were very similar."

Frank rubbed his chin for a moment, thinking hard. "Kong could have gotten that tattoo when he was stationed in Japan."

Joe nodded, a look of intense satisfaction on his face. "Since Kong was in the SEALs, that might explain the commando tactics Blade used to try to kill Buddy. This is all starting to fall into place, Frank."

"I'm beginning to think so, too, but we can't have Kong arrested just on guesswork."

"Then let's talk to someone who knows Kong and who'd know if he has that particular tattoo at his waist," Joe answered. "Like Clare."

"In the coffee shop Jake mentioned that she was staying at the Star-Lite Motel. Let's head over there now. You gather all the photos and any equipment we'll need. I'll get the van warmed up," Frank said decisively.

"What can I do to help?" Callie asked.

"Well, I don't know if you should—" Joe began, but Callie cut him off.

She stood nose to nose with Joe, her fists on her hips. "Joe Hardy, don't give me any of this you-can't-come-because-it's-too-dangerous-for-a-girl stuff. Besides, I can get you in to see Clare without arousing her suspicions. I'll just tell her I want to interview her for my article on Buddy."

"Clare's not exactly wild about discussing Buddy, Callie," Joe insisted.

"She may not talk to you, Joe, but she will respond to the power of the press. Almost everybody wants some kind of recognition. I'll tell Clare the article's about her. I'll flatter her silly if I have to. Whatever it takes!" She shook her finger in Joe's face.

Frank kept out of the discussion. He knew from long experience that Joe's arguments would be futile.

"Give it up, Joe. Admit you're beaten."

Joe smiled and tried to look like a gracious loser, but Frank could tell he was annoyed.

With Joe behind the wheel the three located the Star-Lite Motel in a run-down neighborhood near the arena.

Frank was surprised when he saw how shabby the two-story motel was. It badly needed new siding, and there was garbage scattered all over the parking lot.

"No wonder Jake didn't want his sister staying here," Frank said.

"Really," Joe agreed. "This place is an eyesore."

They parked the van near the front office and went inside. "Where can we find Clare Williams?" Frank asked the unshaven desk clerk.

"Room Twenty-three. Other side of the motel," the clerk replied with a toothless grin.

They drove around to Clare's door and piled out. Before locking the door Frank grabbed his camera and the envelope full of photo enlargements. Callie was in the lead, so she rapped sharply on the door of Room Twenty-three.

They waited for what seemed a very long time before they heard someone coming up to the door. It popped open a crack, and Frank could see Clare's face in the dim light just beyond the door chain.

"Who's there?" she asked.

"It's Callie Shaw, Miss Williams," Callie explained quickly. "I'm a reporter for the Bayport *Examiner*. Can I talk to you for a few minutes?"

"What about?" Clare asked, opening the door a little wider.

"Your influence on Buddy Death's music," Callie answered.

Clare started to slam the door, saying, "No thanks. I'm through talking about that bum!"

Callie stuck her foot in the door and pressed

forward. "Wait, Clare. I've heard about your playing and singing from Joe. I want to talk about the material you've written."

"It's nothing," Clare said, exasperated because Callie kept moving into her room. "Besides," she said wearily, "I'm not really a musician. I'm more of a poet."

As Joe and Frank slipped in behind Callie, Clare gave them a quick once-over.

"Hey, what is this? Look, I'm really not up to having my room invaded by the press right now," she said, running her fingers through her hair. "What are those guys doing here, anyway?"

"They're helping me with my story," Callie said. "I'm sorry if we're intruding, but it's more important than you might realize."

"You might even save Buddy's life," Frank added.

"You think I care what happens to that louse?" Clare said defiantly.

"I think you care a lot," Callie replied softly, "or you wouldn't be following him all over the country on the chance that you'll get to spend five minutes with him."

Clare buried her face in her hands.

"You're right," she said tearfully. "He—he hurt me, but I still care about him. Kong told me about this whole Blade business, and I'm scared for Buddy!"

Callie put her arm around Clare's shoulders.

"Take it easy, Clare. Look, I know a way you can help Buddy right now."

Clare looked up at Callie with red-rimmed eyes. "How?"

Frank stepped over to Clare and handed her the enlargements he'd made. "I took these photos of Blade in the catwalks just after the spotlight missed Buddy. Look at the closeups of the tattoo around Blade's waist and tell us if you can identify it," Frank instructed.

Frank noticed that Clare paled visibly as soon as she glanced at the clearest enlargement of the design.

"Oh, no," she muttered.

"What's wrong?" Joe jumped in.

Clare stared at the trio surrounding her and pointed to the photo in her hand. "Kong has a tattoo like this." Her expression grew more serious, and she added in a quiet voice, "And so does Jake. They got them together in Tokyo."

Callie gently took the photos from Clare's hand and led her to the edge of the bed.

"Clare, you may just have saved Buddy's life," Callie told her. "I'll explain all of this to you soon, but I can't right now. Stay here. Don't call anybody or go out. I'll call you after Buddy's show, okay?"

Clare nodded, stunned.

"I knew it!" Joe said triumphantly as soon

as they were outside Clare's room. "Kong is Blade!"

"Don't jump to any conclusions," Frank warned. "Jake has the same tattoo. We can't go around making rash accusations without better proof!"

"Well, we can at least warn Schacht about our suspicions," Joe said forcefully.

"All right," Frank said. "That's reasonable."

Frank made the call, but when he got through to Schacht's office in the arena he was informed that Mr. Schacht was with Buddy and could not be reached until shortly before the concert. Frank left a message for Schacht to contact the Hardys as soon as possible.

He turned to Joe and Callie with a grim expression. "Schacht's not available. He's got Buddy under wraps."

Frank flicked a glance at his watch. "Let's get to the arena before Buddy and make one last search for Blade."

"If we can surprise Kong, maybe we can 'persuade' him to show us his tattoos," Joe said with a hard expression gleaming in his eyes.

"Let's roll," Frank said impatiently. "Time's wasting, and we're not that much closer to catching Blade."

The trio walked around the corner of the

motel to where Joe had parked the van, and Frank and Callie climbed in.

"Hey, the hood's unlatched!" Joe shouted. "Somebody's been tinkering with our van!"

"Leaving it parked in this neighborhood, it wouldn't surprise me if somebody swiped our battery," Frank said angrily.

Joe stepped quickly over to the van and raised the hood.

Immediately he ran to the door and waved Frank and Callie out of the van.

"What's wrong, Joe?" Frank asked.

"There's a bomb wired to the engine! Both of you get out of the van! *Now!*"

Chapter 15

JOE RAN BACK to look at the compact bundle of plastic explosive wired to the van's battery again. It was a simple, deadly apparatus: Yellow wires that ended in alligator clips were attached to the battery terminals and the starter. It was all designed to explode when the driver started the engine.

Joe's blood ran cold as he thought about what would have happened if he hadn't noticed that the hood was unlatched. They would have been blown to bits.

"Get around the corner and call the cops!" Joe yelled as they took off past him to the corner.

Joe then turned his attention back to the bomb. He traced the two yellow ignition wires to a place under the packet of plastic explosive that was taped to the rear wall of the engine compartment, only a few inches from the cab. Joe gingerly examined the wires, knowing he had to be sure there was no additional time fuse.

Joe slowly reached over to the two alligator clips attached to the battery and unclamped them, letting out a sigh of relief when nothing happened.

Suddenly Frank stuck his head around the corner of the motel. "Bomb squad's on their way. Do you need any help?" Frank called.

"No!" Joe yelled back. "I'm trying to disarm the bomb. Stay back! Get everyone out of the motel!"

"You're crazy," Frank shouted. "Leave it for the pros, Joe!"

"I can't. There's too much stuff here. I think there's a time fuse that'll detonate it automatically if we wait too long," Joe said. He waited until Frank had pulled his head back around the corner, then Joe carefully peeled up the tape from the outer edge and lifted up the packet of explosive to expose the underside.

Joe felt a little chill down his spine as he realized that his hunch had been right. There was a small digital clock and a D battery wired to a blasting cap with a thin wire.

Joe's eyes flicked down to the timer, which

read :05. It changed to :04 as he pulled out his Swiss army knife and flipped open the scissors. The little clock read :03 as Joe put the scissor blades to the ignition wire. It changed to :02 as Joe snipped the wire.

To Joe's horror, the clock kept ticking. But when it hit :00 without the bomb exploding, Joe knew the circuit had been broken. The clock had continued ticking because it was wired directly into the battery.

He carefully lifted the inert bomb off the engine wall and set it on the asphalt beside the van.

"Frank! Callie! All clear!" Joe shouted with relief.

First Frank, then Callie cautiously emerged from around the corner of the motel wall.

"It's okay. I disarmed it," Joe told them with a smile.

"Thanks, Joe," Frank said, punching him lightly on the shoulder. "That took guts!"

Just then Joe saw two Bayport police cruisers and a big van marked Bomb Disposal Unit pull into the Star-Lite parking lot. All three police vehicles braked to a stop just before the corner of the motel.

"What's the story?" Con Riley barked at the Hardys as soon as he jumped out of his police car.

"There was a bomb in our van, Con. I disarmed it," Joe explained.

"You *what?*" Con shouted as the entire bomb squad and three uniformed cops crowded around excitedly.

"I had to," Joe said quickly. "The bomb was wired to a backup fuse and a timer so it would go off automatically unless it was disarmed."

"Let's check this out," the sergeant in charge of the bomb squad ordered. He walked cautiously to the corner, followed by two men from the squad carrying blankets that dampened explosives. They were pulling a little cart that supported a spherical bomb-proof containment chamber.

While the bomb squad investigated for the next hour and a half Joe and Frank were forced to explain to an irate Con Riley what had happened.

"So you see, Con, we thought Blade planted this bomb to stop us from returning to the arena tonight, where he obviously plans another attempt on Buddy Death." Joe spoke rapidly, hoping Con would buy his story.

"I don't know," Con said doubtfully. "I should bring you down to the station house to make a statement."

"But, Con, if you keep us here, that might give Blade enough time to kill Buddy!" Frank said loudly.

"You've got to let us get to the arena!" Joe added.

"You boys are not the law. This is very serious business, and I don't know why I'm letting you stay on the case, but I will. Remember, you're only helpers—not the law. I'm calling for backup. If that nut's inside, we'll find him," Riley asserted.

At that moment the bomb squad came by, pulling their cart.

"It's safe," the sergeant announced.

"The kid did a good job of disarming this baby," one of his men commented.

Joe and Frank thanked the sergeant, then, along with Callie, they piled into their van.

With Frank behind the wheel they drove to the arena, following the screeching siren of Con's police car.

As a uniformed cop waved them in through an emergency entrance Joe noticed that the huge parking lots surrounding the arena were already filled. The excited talking and shouts of the arena crowd mixed with snatches of recorded warm-up music blasting over the sound system.

Con and a squad of cops led the way into tunnel A, with Frank, Joe, and Callie following.

The entrance to the tunnel was jammed shoulder to shoulder with teenagers, many wearing Buddy Death Band T-shirts and black leather pants. The atmosphere was electric. Joe heard crazy laughter and shouting all around him. As he pushed through a close-packed group of teens he couldn't help noticing one long-haired fan playing air guitar in sync with the rock music that pounded through the mammoth sound system at an almost earsplitting level. The would-be musician was totally oblivious to the squad of Bayport cops that was pushing toward the bowl of the arena.

Tex, who stood near the entrance of tunnel A, tossed a walkie-talkie to both Frank and Joe as soon as he saw them. Tex looked sweaty and totally frazzled.

"Where've you guys been? It's six-thirty. Jake's fit to be tied!" Tex said anxiously.

"I can't worry about that!" Frank shouted. "Where can we find Schacht?"

"I don't know where anybody is!" Tex raised his voice to be heard over the racket. "I haven't been able to raise Kong or Jake on their walkie-talkies for a while. I can't get Bobby Mellor, either! I'm swamped, boys!"

"If you see Schacht, tell him we have to talk!" Joe shouted.

Tex nodded, then turned and pushed his way through the crowd of fans to the stage, which was guarded by a ring of muscular bouncers dressed in black Buddy Death security T-shirts and jeans.

"If Blade is out in the open, maybe we can bag him quietly before the show starts," Joe shouted to Frank.

"Somehow I don't think Blade is the type to come quietly," Frank shouted back, smiling grimly.

For the next hour or so Frank and Joe checked out the arena floor. They came up empty.

They flashed their crew badges to gain admittance to the backstage area next. Buddy's motor home had been driven directly behind the stage. The two bodyguards stood on either side of the motor home's door, their eyes moving constantly to scan the area for any sign of danger.

A small trailer had been set up next to it as a temporary office, and a steady stream of roadies, cops, and arena security guards flowed in and out of it.

"Unless I miss my guess," Joe observed, "that is where we'll find Syd Schacht."

Joe led the way into the cramped trailer, where they found Schacht seated behind a makeshift desk talking on a telephone and mopping his brow. As soon as he caught sight of the Hardys he abruptly hung up on whomever he'd been talking to.

"Am I glad to see you guys," Schacht said with relief. "What's up?"

"There's no time to explain now," Joe said breathlessly, "but we need to know where Jake and Kong are."

"Jake's working with the special effects

gear in the catwalks,'' Schacht replied. ''As for Kong, the big goon disappeared. Where do you think Blade will strike?'' he asked anxiously.

''If he follows his past pattern, it's likely he'll strike from above,'' Frank replied.

''I agree,'' Joe said. ''Backstage is crawling with cops and guards. It'd be much easier for him to get at Buddy from above, so that's where we'll be standing watch.''

''While you guys do that I think I'll join the press corps. I still have a story to get out,'' Callie told Frank. ''And don't forget my exclusive, Mr. Schacht,'' she called over her shoulder as she headed off toward the crowd of press people. Joe saw her pull out her press pass and clip it onto her blouse.

''If we bag Blade, she'll probably get a Pulitzer prize,'' Frank joked.

''Come on, Frank,'' Joe said, hurrying out the trailer door toward the backstage ladders that went up to the catwalks.

He noticed Buddy coming out of the trailer and joining the rest of his band. He was relieved to see Sammy up and around, though he did look almost as pale as Buddy was naturally. Skeezer stood behind Sammy, leaning against an equipment case.

Eric seemed to be extremely worried as he waited near Sammy and Skeezer, his blue electric guitar strapped across his chest.

By the time Joe and Frank reached the ladders to climb up to the catwalks the audience had been let in and was chanting for Buddy. Recorded intro music continued to blare out, but as the boys climbed into the flies it ceased. Spotlights blasted pinwheels of multicolored light in all directions for twenty minutes. Then finally, at showtime, the smoke machines kicked in, creating a thick wall of smoke through which Buddy and the other band members would suddenly appear. There was no opening band for the group. Joe thought Buddy would be jealous of the competition.

As Joe groped his way along the catwalk with the crazy light from the spotlights strobing below him, red laser beams suddenly began hissing all around.

Involuntarily, Joe ducked and then flattened himself to the deck of the swaying catwalk. Finally he realized that the laser beams were part of the show and not an attack launched by Blade. He sneaked a look behind him and saw that Frank had done the same thing, so he didn't feel so foolish.

"Nervous?" Joe quipped.

"Very funny," Frank said sourly. "I noticed you went down first, though."

"Better safe than sorry," Joe said as he got back to his feet.

"If Blade is going to strike, he probably won't try anything until Buddy hits the stage,"

Frank yelled over the roar of the crowd as Eric and Skeezer appeared onstage. Sammy came on moments later, timing his entrance so that he began his drum roll just as the smoke was clearing across the stage.

"I agree," Joe shouted back. "But where do we start looking?"

A bright spotlight suddenly slashed across a small special effects platform directly over the stage. Joe and Frank both scanned it automatically for signs of danger. Joe started in surprise when he spotted a dark form hunched over a compressed-air cannon normally used to fire confetti over the crowd.

"Frank, do you see him?" he shouted over the electric guitars and thrumming drums.

"It's Blade! He's doing something to the cannon. We've got to stop him!" Frank shouted.

Joe saw the dark figure putting handfuls of something glittery into the barrel of the cannon. He swiveled it around and pointed it down directly at the stage. The electric guitars rose to a raucous wail, and then Buddy leapt into the spotlight to stand center stage at the edge of the apron.

"He's right in the cannon's sights!" Joe shouted.

Chapter 16

FRANK RAN as fast as he dared on the swaying catwalk. The special effects platform where Blade stood was still thirty feet away.

Up ahead he saw Joe snatch something from an open toolbox one of the roadies had left sitting on top of a speaker cabinet suspended next to the catwalk. A moment later Joe stopped moving abruptly, and Frank was just able to avoid running into his back.

Joe braced his feet in a pitcher's stance and hurled a silver crescent wrench at Blade with all his might. Frank thought Joe's aim was bad, because the wrench missed Blade and slammed into the back of the cannon, knocking it down and swinging the barrel up. He hadn't been aiming for Blade after all. With a grunt muffled by his black mask Blade swiveled the cannon around to face the Hardys. Then he thumbed the cannon's electric trigger.

Boom!

The cannon fired a second after the Hardys hit the deck again. As Frank hugged the catwalk he heard small missiles whizzing overhead.

After a moment Frank risked a peek and saw that the black canvas covering over the catwalks was studded with winged metal darts. Frank shuddered when he thought of what the little darts would have done to him. Or to Buddy. But before Blade had a chance to reload Frank was up and charging toward the platform.

Since he and Joe were running at full speed toward the only ladder that led to the small effects platform, Frank figured they had to have Blade cornered. He realized how wrong he was a moment later when Blade whipped a stubby pistol from his belt and fired it—not at the Hardys, as Frank had expected, but at a crossbeam over the stage. The pistol fired with a loud report, shooting out a small grappling hook attached to a light nylon line.

As Joe and Frank hurried along the catwalk above the special effects platform Blade wrapped the line around his right wrist and swung to a section of catwalk over the opposite side of the stage.

"He won't get away!" Frank insisted, putting his walkie-talkie up to his mouth. "The cops can surround the stage right now!"

"Con Riley, over. This is Frank Hardy! Blade is here! He's on the east side catwalk—" Frank paused while he listened to Con's instructions. "All right," Frank agreed. "Your men will surround the stage, and we'll drive him down to you."

Frank turned back to Joe. "Where's Blade now?"

"Still over the stage, on the catwalk," Joe said, pointing. "What's the plan?" he asked.

"Con's giving us one chance before he sends his boys up here. He doesn't want the crowd to panic," Frank replied.

"What if Blade doubles back on us?"

"Then it's up to us to stop him," Frank replied with a grim set to his jaw. "You go ahead, Joe. Keep Blade busy."

"And where will you be?" Joe asked.

"I'm going back to prepare a few surprises for Blade."

Moving fast, Frank found the roadie's toolbox on the speaker and pulled out the pliers and other things he knew he'd need, then returned to the spot where the side catwalk intersected with the catwalk that bisected the dome.

He stretched a four-foot length of piano wire at ankle height between the two upright supports just before the intersection, then he strung another piece chest-high.

Before leaving, Frank sprayed some slippery lubricant on the deck of the catwalk about two feet in front of the wires. He hoped his booby trap would catch Blade off guard.

Frank quickly booby-trapped the catwalk on the opposite side of the arena as well, then sprayed the lubricant on the deck behind him and hurried along the catwalk to meet Joe.

To his horror, Frank saw Joe grappling with Blade on the catwalk that ran over the width of the backstage area.

"Hey!" he yelled.

Frank raced along the catwalk toward them, his running causing it to rock perilously.

Joe and Blade were locked in a battle of strength. Blade had Joe's left wrist, and Joe held on to Blade's right wrist for dear life, trying to keep Blade's stubby pistol pointed away from him.

Joe and Blade were dancing in a tight circle as Blade slid his foot behind Joe's ankle with snakelike speed. Joe went over backward, and Blade pulled his gun hand free.

Frank felt a cold ball of fear in his stomach as Blade lowered his pistol to point it right at Joe's head. Frank ran headlong down the catwalk, heedless of the danger, screaming, *"No-o-o-o!"*

Blade glanced up, and his pistol wavered between the two brothers, which gave Frank time to pull the pliers from his back pocket and throw them at Blade.

The pliers struck Blade's wrist, knocking the stubby gun from his grip, sending it tumbling over the edge of the catwalk.

At the same moment Joe grabbed Blade's left ankle and pulled it out from under him. Frank watched as Joe pounced on Blade like a tiger, pinning him to the deck.

Blade quickly pushed Joe off with a tremendous heave just as Frank arrived. Joe stumbled backward into Frank, who teetered on the edge of the catwalk, desperately trying to regain his balance.

Frank snagged a guy wire with one hand. A split second later Joe grabbed his other hand and pulled him to the center of the catwalk.

The boys looked around for Blade and saw him sprinting down the catwalk.

"He's getting away again!" Joe yelled.

"He won't get far," Frank assured him as he took off after Blade.

Far ahead of him Frank watched as Blade suddenly ran into an invisible barrier, then slid over the edge of the catwalk.

Blade managed to snag the edge of the catwalk as he fell.

"Take it easy," Frank cautioned as he edged over to Blade's gloved fingers.

"Stay back or I'll let go!" Blade threatened.

"I wouldn't do that," Frank said tensely, edging closer to his hands.

"I won't be taken alive," Blade shouted.

"Oh, yes, you will, *Jake!*" Frank shouted, and dived over his booby trap to make a grab for Jake's hands. The surprise of being recognized kept Jake from reacting for a second. In that last possible instant Frank caught his hand.

"Help me pull him up, Joe," Frank urged through gritted teeth.

A few hours later, after the concert was over, Frank, Joe, and Callie were sitting in Schacht's office trailer with Schacht, Con Riley, and Captain Hubbard.

The flood of relief Frank had felt after capturing Blade had left him about an hour earlier, and he just felt tired. He glanced at his watch, wondering when Con would let them go. He and Joe had explained almost every aspect of Blade's crimes.

"I still don't see how you knew Jake Williams was Blade, Frank," Con Riley was saying.

"Well, he wasn't our only suspect, but when I saw him fighting with Joe on the catwalk I realized Jake had to be Blade because Kong would be too tall."

"Whatever happened to Kong, anyway?" Joe inquired.

Captain Hubbard chuckled, "I found the big galoot bound and gagged in a storage closet. He'd found Williams while he was getting into his Blade outfit, so Williams decked him, then tied him up."

"Did you get a motive for his attempts on Buddy?" Callie asked.

"Maybe I can explain that," Clare said quietly. "Jake did it for me. He—he's not really bad, he just thought he had to stick up for his little sister."

"But why try to kill Buddy?" Joe asked her.

"Because Buddy stole my poems. You see, I had a notebook full of poems that I'd been writing ever since I was a little girl. I showed it to Buddy when we were dating, and he really liked them. Then, after he dumped me, I went to look for my notebook, and it was gone. I found out later that Buddy had stolen it."

"Do you know that for a fact?" Frank inquired.

Clare nodded sadly. "The first time I heard Buddy's album I already knew all the lyrics because they were from my poems. But because Buddy had stolen my book there was no way I could prove it.

"Jake felt totally frustrated about the way Buddy had gotten away with hurting me and stealing my poems. I guess he wanted revenge and knew only one way to get it."

Clare's voice fell off, and she stared down at her lap. An awkward silence fell over the group for a moment until Con Riley broke in.

"Well, we're almost finished if you'll just bear with me, people," he said, opening his notebook to a fresh page. "I'm still fuzzy on how Blade—er, Williams—performed his acts of sabotage."

Frank sighed. "It was easy. Jake was the special effects supervisor. He had access to all the equipment. All he had to do was walk a little way down the catwalk, loosen four bolts, and *bang*—down comes the light. It was easy for him to rig the mike stand to electrocute someone."

"Yeah, and he used Kong to decoy Mellor away from the limo just long enough so he could sabotage the brakes," Joe put in. "The guy is definitely a mechanical wizard. In a lot of ways his special effects work was great training for this. Real life—real murder—is a lot simpler than faking it."

"But how did he know when Buddy's lunch was coming up so he could poison it?" Con asked.

"What I suspect is that Jake hid somewhere in the hotel, eavesdropping on Buddy's room phone with that lineman's handset I saw," Frank explained. "When Buddy ordered the food Jake disguised himself as a waiter, slipped into the kitchen, and did his dirty work."

"Okay, I'll buy that," Con said. "But why do you think he tried to blow you two up?"

"Panic. He knew he was running out of time to kill Buddy, and Frank and I had spoiled his plans several times. He got careless, too. That bomb might have killed his sister as well as us, but at that point Jake wasn't thinking too clearly.

"One of the things that made me suspicious of Bobby Mellor initially was that life insurance policy he had on Buddy," Joe said thoughtfully.

Schacht dismissed that with a wave of his hand. "Insuring your star's life is a standard practice in this business. There's nothing mysterious about it."

Frank grinned at Joe. "Didn't I tell you that before?"

Joe was annoyed. "Well, I wouldn't have been so suspicious of Mellor if the guy had a normal past. His past ended after five years. That's pretty strange."

Schacht chuckled. "You boys are pretty thorough," he said admiringly. "Bobby's past only goes back five years because Mellor's not his real name. He ditched his old identity after a partner of his ran out on him and left him with a lot of bad debts and his reputation in tatters. He's been rebuilding and repairing ever since."

"Well, that explains a lot," Joe said, satisfied.

"Say, what would you say to joining my outfit permanently? I could use a couple of bright boys like you."

Frank and Joe exchanged grins, then looked at Schacht and shook their heads.

"No thanks, Mr. Schacht," Frank said with a smile. "I think we'll stick to being detectives. Being a roadie is too much like work!"

Frank and Joe's next case:

Frank, Joe, and Callie are off to Virginia City, Nevada, heart of the Comstock Lode, to visit Callie's friend Kerry Prescott. Kerry's father, Ted, has developed a system to extract new gold from old mines—but the deeper Ted digs, the more danger he finds. Someone means to put him down for good!

Gold fever is running high, and lives are at stake. But Frank and Joe stake a claim of their own: they're out to put a stop to a gold-digging, gun-toting gang of desperadoes. The Hardys head for a showdown eighty feet underground, where they discover just how wild the Wild West can be . . . in *Dirty Deeds,* Case #49 in The Hardy Boys Casefiles™.